MYTHICAL UNIVERSITY
The Golden Scrolls

NOVA KIRSCH

Independently Published
COLORADO

Welcome to

Social Media Platforms
FB: @MythicalUniversity, @NovaKirsch
Twitter: @IamNovaKirsch
Instagram: @Unistangs, @IamNovaKirsch
Website: https://www.MythicalUniversity.com
Merchandise: https://shop.MythicalUniversity.com

Copyright © 2023 by Christopher Novak writing as Nova Kirsch

All rights reserved - Independently Published

No part of this publication may be reproduced, stored in a retrieval system, or transmitted in any form by any means, electronic, mechanical, photocopying, recording, or otherwise, without written permission of the publisher.

**For information regarding permissions visit:
www.NovaKirsch.com**

This book is a work of fiction. Names, characters, places, and incidents are either the product of the author's imagination or are used fictitiously, and any resemblance to actual persons, living or dead, business establishments, events, or locals is entirely coincidental.

First printing: 2023

Thank you to AD and MR for the feedback
Edited by Tanya Novak
Book cover design, characters, concept, story, and artwork by Christopher Novak

This book is dedicated to those who refuse to give up on their search of who they really want to become

People will tell you no or that you can't do it
Remember, it's not up to them
You just need to

Table of Contents

Chapter 1 Taking On The Snoads 1
Chapter 2 King Olly 12
Chapter 3 Inside The Castle Walls 29
Chapter 4 Understanding the Past 49
Chapter 5 The Magic Words 71
Chapter 6 Kennz's Vision 95
Chapter 7 Now We Know Where It Is 108
Chapter 8 Proving Her Wrong 117
Chapter 9 The Other Side of the Door 149
Chapter 10 Not What I Had Expected 170
Chapter 11 It's Not Black or White 182
Chapter 12 Confronting My Past 189
Chapter 13 The Journals 200
Chapter 14 The Council Code 225
Chapter 15 Jax's Tree: House of Deception 232
Chapter 16 Putting It All Together 258
Chapter 17 The Second To Last Scroll 286
Sneak Peek The Council of Trust 302

Chapter 1 Taking On The Snoads

After we broke our huddle, we decided it would be best to change into our forms. This way we would be better protected and ready for whatever comes our way. Unfortunately, we didn't stay in our forms for very long. Upon entering Margot's tree, only she was still able to retain her Spidox form while the rest of us automatically changed back into our human forms.

"That is strange," Allie thought. She tried changing back into Owl but was unsuccessful. "Why can't we keep our forms?"

"Her tree…her rules," Jax quipped.

Chapter 1 Taking On The Snoads

"I don't think it works that way, Jax. Yes, her tree, but I don't think the rules were set by her," I replied.

"Then whose rules are we playing by?" he asked.

"I have a feeling mine. Again, just not sure why."

Upon entering the tree, it's almost as if we were transported to a different world and time. Although things somewhat resembled Forest Creek, they appeared to be from a different time and place.

"Where are we?" Kennz asked, looking around. "Is this Forest Creek? It looks so young."

Spidox went running ahead and then motioned for us to all stop. She was sensing something but wasn't quite sure what it was. The rest of us started to hear what sounded like clacking noises. We each turned a different direction seeing creatures bounding through the forest.

"What are those things?" Mylo asked.

"I have no idea, but let's not stand around and find out," I told him and the others.

We were ready to take off running when these creatures landed all around us encircling us like prey with their weapons pointed right at us. They appeared to be an army of snails but had the legs of toads.

I looked at them and then it dawned on me what they were. I remember Z giving us a little history lesson one time. "Are you snoads?" I curiously asked.

Either they didn't understand me, I got it wrong, or they just didn't want me to speak as their weapons drew closer to us.

"I'll stop talking, now," I said.

Chapter 1 Taking On The Snoads

One of the snoads used his weapon and motioned for us to move walking away from where we were. It was just the five of us since Spidox was a little ways from us, but still able to see what was going on and then trailed us keeping out of sight.

While we were walking Allie quietly asked if I could summon my horn or staff. "I've tried. It's like nothing will work for me here," I whispered to her.

"I tried transforming, but couldn't," Allie said back to me.

The snoads kept us walking by poking their weapons at us and pushing us along. I was able to get a glance at Jax and Mylo but they had multiple snoads around them with weapons pointed directly at them. I could feel something lightly tugging at my shirt. I dismissed it at first until I felt it again. I subtly turned my head and saw Kennz slightly turn her head and eyes to the left of us. Spidox had been following us and was now to our left using the trees and bushes to hide from the snoads.

We kept this pace and then were forced to stop. One of the snoads motioned for us to look up a bit. Just ahead of us, along the side of one of the peaks was a mini castle – not that it was tiny in stature, it just wasn't as large and extravagant as a normal looking castle. It was also covered in moss. I'm thinking this is where the leader of the snoads was. I was just hoping that Spidox could figure something out before we had the privilege and opportunity of visiting him or her. I didn't really feel like being invited for dinner – knowing that we would probably be the dinner. And, since none of us could use any of our abilities, I knew we were no match for the weapons they had drawn on us.

Chapter 1 Taking On The Snoads

Our only hope was Spidox. I'm hopeful she thinks of something quick since it's close to dinnertime. I don't think any of us really want to be their main course tonight.

I looked towards Spidox and she gave me some sort of a signal and then took off towards the castle. Since I wasn't able to speak to the others, there was no way for me to ask if anyone else had seen Spidox take off ahead of us.

She quickly made her way staying near the path, but still out of sight from the snoads. The path wasn't straightforward. It had a few twists and turns to it leading up the side of the peak. The castle wasn't too far up it and wasn't really protected. There was no moat or even a drawbridge to cross. The castle was exposed with the exception of the moss growing on it. This made me wonder if these were the only creatures here or if this was a fairly friendly land and time, and there was no need for the protection. I then looked at the weapons they were holding and had second thoughts. Their weapons were like giant pitchforks except with multiple points to each fork. It's almost like there were more tiny pitch forks at the end of each fork...if that makes sense.

The snoads kept us moving forward, standing on their hind legs hopping as they went. A few times I could feel the hard shells of the guardsmen in front of me. I was trying to time my steps with the length of their hops but mistimed them a few times.

The closer we got to the castle the more I kept looking for Spidox. I knew she was up to something, I just didn't know what it was. Just then Kennz tugged at my shirt somewhat gently, again. I glanced her way and saw her sneakily

Chapter 1 Taking On The Snoads

pointing towards the castle; in particular above the portcullis. Spidox was suspended from her webbing waiting for the snoads and us to get closer. I'm hoping that the others saw what Kennz and I had seen so they knew to expect something. Just not sure what that something will be.

We reached the point on the path than now led directly to the castle doors. I looked above them but could no longer see Spidox. Instead, I saw something that looked like a giant net – ready to capture it's prey. Just then a rock-like projectile came hurling towards one of the snoad guardsmen knocking him to the ground. Spidox had spun her webbing so tight that it was as hard as a rock. She then made her presence known. She was now sitting on top of the castle perched high upon one of the battlements armed, mind you six of them, with different objects. The snoads took note of this and quickly ran towards her leaving the one downed snoad. They scurried towards the portcullis. Upon arriving at the castle door, Spidox hurled something towards her netting causing it to fall on top of the other snoad guardsmen. The netting instantly captured them making it impossible for them to escape. We ran towards them and quickly snatched their weapons from them now being armed ourselves.

"Great job, Spidox!" I yelled up to her.

She quickly ballooned down to us.

"Thank you," she said turning back into her human form.

"Margot, do you know this place?" Allie asked her.

"I don't. At least not that I can remember and nothing looks familiar to me. It looks like Forest Creek, just a different time," she answered.

Chapter 1 Taking On The Snoads

"What is this place?" Mylo asked.

"I think it's a castle," chuckled Jax.

"You think, bro?" Mylo said shaking his head at Jax. "I mean if this is Forest Creek, then where has this castle been the entire time?"

We looked at it and then at the surroundings. "I'm not sure what ever happened to it, but I bet that we're going to find out. I do get a feeling that what we are searching for is probably within these castle walls," I told them.

"I think you're right," Margot said. "I'm just not sure what to expect once we get in there."

"Whatever we decide to do we better do it quick," Jax said.

"Why?" I asked.

"Because more of those creatures are coming right for us," he said, pointing towards the other side of the castle.

Margot was about to change into Spidox when I stopped her.

"There's too many of them for you to take on by yourself. Since we can't change, I think it would be best if we can get inside. We might stand a better chance in there," I told her.

"We might also be able to find out more about the snoads and what this place is," said Allie.

"And maybe when we are," I started. "because I don't think we're in Kansas anymore, guys."

CHAPTER 2 KING OLLY

Jax noticed a rope leading to the castle door. "I bet if we can release the rope the door will open," he said.

"No time for that," Margot said, quickly changing to Spidox.

She quickly made some web projectiles and hurled them in the direction of the charging snoads, landing them in front of them.

"I think you missed," Jax told her.

The snoads hopped on top of them and quickly stopped in their tracks due to the stickiness of the webbing. Spidox looked at Jax.

"I stand corrected," he told her.

Spidox then cast out six long narrow webbings towards the top of the castle door, just long enough for each of us to take hold of. "Each of you grab an end and help me pull the door open," she told us.

We threw the weapons down before grabbing hold of the webbing. Even though there was no moat around the castle, this was your typical drawbridge that we had to open. The webbing was sticky and there was no way it was coming loose from the door. We each grabbed one of the ends before Spidox stopped us.

"Wait just a second," she blurted. She threw a web towards the captured snoads. She then pulled them away from where the door would have landed so they wouldn't become squished snoads. She threw an extra layer of webbing over the top of them making sure they would stay entangled in it for a while.

Chapter 2 King Olly

"Okay...on the count of three," Spidox started. "One, two, three...pull!" she yelled out.

With all of our might we pulled on the door trying to draw it open. It took a few seconds, but we were finally able to get the door to come on down.

"That's one heavy door!" exclaimed Mylo.

"We're not done with it, yet!" Spidox exclaimed.

"What do you mean?" Allie asked her.

"Once we get inside we're going to have to pull it closed," she answered.

We didn't even bother picking the weapons back up; instead, we ran across the door entering the castle. Spidox then cast out six more long narrow webbings and this time we didn't wait for her to count. We pulled even harder slowly backing our way into the castle. It took more effort and tugging on our part but we were able to get the door closed back up.

The five of us shook our arms out to get rid of some of the tightness we just experienced. Spidox was shaking out six of hers.

"Whoa! Look at this place," uttered Mylo.

It was magnificent looking inside. There were statues of what appeared to be famous looking snoad generals from yesteryear all standing valiantly. The statues looked like they were made out of some sort of a metal that none of us recognized. Mylo went up to one of them and touched it. He pressed on it a little too hard making it wobble. Spidox threw a web at it and pulled it back rebalancing it.

"How about we don't touch anything in here unless we absolutely have too," I told everyone.

Chapter 2 King Olly

"Good idea," Jax said, elbowing Mylo when he walked back towards us.

"What? I wanted to see what it felt like," Mylo proclaimed.

"Well?" Jax asked him.

"Well what?" Mylo asked back.

"What did it feel like?" Jax asked right back.

"Oh, yeah. Well, it felt weird...almost gushy like," answered Mylo.

Spidox turned back into Margot and then said, "When I threw my webs at it, it didn't feel that way."

We looked at Mylo.

"What? I'm serious. It was gushy. If you don't believe me, go feel it for yourself," he confidently said.

Margot walked over to it and put her hands on it. "This is weird. It is gushy. What is this stuff?"

"It's made from bojo berries and you're all trespassing," a familiar voice yelled out to us.

We turned around quickly, all being taken aback that someone else was in the room. We not only were surprised to hear a familiar voice, but to also see someone we knew.

"Dad?" Margot remarked. "You look so young and all dressed in red. What are you doing here?"

"Dad? I don't know you young lady. Who sent you? Was it those morpions again trying to sneak in more of their moles?" he asked us.

"But you're my dad. You're also the War Fox."

"What is a war fox? I am King Olly, leader

Chapter 2 King Olly

of the snoads and you are all trespassing. Plus, I don't appreciate you leaving your symbols around the castle. Are these the new symbols of the morpions?" asked King Olly.

"You're not a snoad, you're the…" Margot started to say when King Olly transformed into a mighty looking snoad. His legs were that of a toad and his back was protected with a very large and red shell.

"Never mind what I was saying," replied Margot.

"Well this just took an interesting turn," said Allie.

I looked at Margot and said, "At least now I know why you thought your father was the Mysterious Man in Red before." I then turned my attention to whomever it was that was standing in our presence. "Sir or King, however you would like us to address you. Would it be possible if you could show us these symbols you are referencing?" I kindly asked him.

"You should know what they are, morpion. You and your kind put them in here. I just don't know how," he told me. "We will not be intimidated any longer. I have assembled an army and we will fight."

"If that's his army, then they are in trouble," Jax whispered to Mylo.

"Quiet, Jax," I told him. "Sir, we are not looking to fight. We are looking for a relic of sorts. I believe these symbols you are talking about will lead us to it. I promise you, we are not looking to harm you or your people in any way and we are not morpions."

Just then the castle door was opened with the snoad army rushing in. "There they are. Those

Chapter 2 King Olly

are the ones who trapped us and hurt one of our guardsman," one of them said.

"Okay...let me rephrase what I just said about not wanting to harm you or your people," I started.

"I'm listening," King Olly said while summoning a weird looking staff and staring at us intently.

"We didn't intentionally hurt anyone," I started, when one of the guardsmen interrupted me.

"Where is the one that was throwing projectiles at us and knocked out one of our guards?"

"Okay...maybe just the one time, but they were coming after us and we were just defending ourselves," I told him.

"Maybe you should stop talking," Allie told me.

"I think I will," I responded.

"Take them to the dungeon. Once you have them locked away go find the one that took out one of my guards. She will be my dinner tonight," King Olly proclaimed.

I quickly looked at Margot and motioned for her to not change. "Sir, we will go in peace if you let us go right now," I told him.

"The only place you will be going is the dungeon. And once we capture the other, you can personally watch me devour her. That will be my treat to you," he told us before motioning to his guardsmen. "Take them to the dungeon and go find me my dinner."

The snoads drew their weapons poking us to start walking. They led us towards the stairs. While we were walking I spotted one of the symbols on an adjacent wall right before we got to

Chapter 2 King Olly

the stairs. There was another one at the bottom of them, too.

Once we reached the bottom of the stairs we could see a holding cell. We were forcefully pushed into it by the guardsmen. Before leaving us there, one of them shut the door and locked it. They then hung the key up on the wall opposite where we were, which was about twenty or so feet from us.

"We'll be back for you all shortly after we capture your spider companion," one of them told us.

They headed back to the steps and ascended upwards.

"Why is your dad a snoad, if he really is your dad?" Allie asked Margot.

"He does look a lot like him...except for the snoad part and being a lot younger," Kennz said.

"I have no idea. I'm finding this out like all of you are. It's news to me, too," responded Margot.

I sat down on the only bench inside the cell thinking.

"Are you trying to figure a way out of here?" Mylo asked.

"No. We'll be out shortly. Spidox will get us out of here. I'm trying to puzzle this through about Margot's father. He said something a little strange. Did anyone else pick up on it?" I asked.

I looked at the others and they were shaking their heads no while looking at each other.

"I don't think we did. What did you hear?" Margot asked.

"He called you 'she'. How did he know that Spidox was a her?" I remarked.

Chapter 2 King Olly

"So, you really believe that he is Margot's dad?" Allie asked.

"I think so. I just can't figure out how or why he no longer is a snoad and how he became the War Fox. And what happened to the snoads? Where did they go before I apparently invited them back to Forest Creek?"

"What do you mean 'what happened to them'?" Jax asked.

I looked at the others while they were intently awaiting my explanation. "Give me a few minutes to try and think this through," I told them. I started walking around the room with my hand to my head and then chin trying to remember anything I could.

"She eerily looks like Wesam and Legend when she does that," mentioned Allie.

"I think I've got something," I yelled out. "It's starting to make somewhat sense to me the more I think about it."

"What is?" Margot curiously asked.

"I think we can all agree that we are back at Forest Creek – at least the mythical part of it that regulars can't see,"

"Okay...where are you going with this?" Allie asked.

"Well, if what I am thinking is correct, then I think I know why I invited the snoads to return to Forest Creek. I think I'm starting to remember a little about this place."

"Were you here before?" asked Margot.

"No," I told her.

"Then how are you remembering this place if you were never here?" Allie asked.

Chapter 2 King Olly

"I saw the symbols on the walls. Did anyone else see them?"

The others looked at one another and shook their heads no. "We didn't see any symbols. Are those the ones King Olly accused us of putting here?" asked Jax.

"They're actually the new symbol of the school that my horn changed. I'm just not sure how they got here or if they were already here but looked different how they changed. Seeing them sparked a few memories for me about Forest Creek's past…at least the mythical part of it."

"How far in the past are we talking about?" asked Margot.

"I'm not sure how far in the past we are, Margot. Let's get out of here and see if we can find anymore of those symbols. Hopefully, they will spark more memories for me and we can understand what happened here."

Margot then did her hybrid change into Spidox only having her pedipalps showing. She shot a web over to the keys and latched on to them. She quickly pulled them back in where she used them to undo the lock. After we got out of the cell she closed the door, locked it up, and then threw the keys into the cell towards the very back covering them with a few layers of her webbing.

"That should keep them busy trying to get to them," Margot said, laughing a bit.

"Where do we go now?" Allie asked.

"I don't think we should go back upstairs. Let's explore down here and see what we can find," I told her. "Maybe there are more of the symbols on the walls. Keep an eye out for anything that

Chapter 2 King Olly

may be of interest, except for you Margot, you can keep all four," I said, smiling at her.

With that we left the area of the holding cell and walked in the opposite direction of the stairs towards the other side of the room.

Chapter 3 Inside The Castle Walls

There was a passageway of sorts at the other end of the room that we spotted. Allie stopped about halfway there and just stared at it. We stopped alongside her and looked curiously at her.

"What is it, Allie?" I asked her.

"I don't know. There is just something strangely familiar about it," she said.

"Like what?"

"Not sure, but it's like I've seen it before."

I looked at it for a few moments. "It looks like every other hallway to me," I told her.

Allie walked towards it. The closer she got to it the more she became curious.

Chapter 3 Inside The Castle Walls

"Hey, guys. Come here," she told us, motioning for us to come over.

"What is it, Allie?" Kennz asked her.

"Look down this corridor."

"What about it?" asked Jax.

"I think this is one of the corridors that led through the peak where Spritz and I were taken."

I looked back at the room we were just in. "Hold on…" I said walking back towards the center of it. I then stopped and closed my eyes.

"What is she doing?" Mylo asked in a quiet voice to Jax.

"I have no idea. Just let her go with it."

"Allie, come over here," I called to her.

"What is it, Nia?" she asked, walking to where Nia was standing.

"Look towards the corridor."

Allie looked that direction. "What about it?"

"I think you're onto something about this place. I think this is the very room you were in. Picture a door where that corridor begins. I bet that is the entrance into this room. And, if we follow the corridor, I bet it will take us near to where the college is...or will be just like we traveled before."

"That's crazy!" Allie exclaimed.

"I have a question," said Margot.

"What is it, Margot?" I asked.

"Are you telling us that this is the same room that Allie and Spritz were in? If so, that means the morpion lived here. What happened to the castle because it wasn't here when we rescued Allie?"

"Before anyone answers that I have a question," said Allie. "Nia, didn't Z tell us that the

Chapter 3 Inside The Castle Walls

snoads were water creatures. If that is correct, why isn't there water around the castle or, better yet, why isn't their castle near a lake or water of some sort?"

I didn't know quite how to answer them. "Those are both very good questions and ones that we should probably figure out some other time. Honestly guys, I have no idea. Something doesn't feel right to me. I think we might need to speak with King Olly and find out a little bit more about this place and why they are defending themselves against the morpions."

"Do you really think that is a good idea?" Margot asked. "You know he is wanting me captured and eventually put me on a skewer and devour me."

"If that's what he wants then I say we give it to him," I told her.

"Excuse me!" exclaimed Margot. "I don't think so. How about offering your Unistang form and see which one he chooses?"

"Margot, you're going to be fine. I think we need to take this corridor and see what we can find. After that we'll come back and talk with the king, but it will be on our terms, not his. I figure if we can get him alone then you can use your web of magic against him and we can get the answers we need," I explained.

"Whew! For a moment there I thought you had lost it," Margot said.

"One problem," Jax yelled out.

"What's the issue?" I asked him.

"The corridor gets pretty dark fairly quick. I don't see any kind of light around and you can't summon your horn."

Chapter 3 Inside The Castle Walls

"That could be a problem," I said. "Well now what do we do?"

No one said anything for a few moments until we saw Kennz walking around the room. That's when she finally spoke up and asked, "Hey, guys...what's this on the wall?"

We walked over to where she was and noticed the school symbol, but it was turned upside down. All of us pivoted our heads to the side trying to see it right-side-up...I guess.

"Why is it upside down?" Allie asked, still with her head tilted.

"I have no idea," I answered, with my head tilted.

"Can we turn our heads the right way? Mine's starting to hurt," Margot said.

We turned our heads to their natural position and continued to stare at the symbol. I was curious about it so I put my hand near it to see if anything would happen. Right before I was ready to touch it Spidox shot my hand with her webbing and quickly pulled it away from the symbol.

"What was that for?" I asked her.

Spidox turned back into Margot and pointed to the floor. "This looks like the outline of a trap door."

We slowly backed away from where we were, getting beyond the outer part of the trap door.

"Isn't anyone else curious if that's what really would happen if the symbol was pressed?" asked Kennz.

We were all like little children dying to find out and really wanted to press it. "Margot, could you shoot a piece of your webbing from here and see if it opens it up?"

Chapter 3 Inside The Castle Walls

"I can do that," she answered transforming one arm. She then flung a perfect shot hitting the symbol with one of her webs, but nothing happened. She hit it again, but with the same result.

"I think we're going to have to touch it in order to activate it," Margot said.

"I think you're right, but that means we have to be standing over the door to do it," I replied.

"That's it!" exclaimed Allie. "Nia, can be standing over the door to activate it. Spidox just needs to create a platform so if the door opens Nia will still be above it."

"Good thinking, Allie. Margot, how quick can you create a platform of webbing?"

Margot went full on Spidox and within a matter of seconds a platform was created above the trap door that looked sturdy enough for me and probably everyone else in the room to stand on.

"Right on. This will work," I told her. I walked on top of the platform and, before touching the symbol, I looked at the others. "Here goes nothing," I said touching my hand to the symbol.

The symbol glowed and, sure enough, the trap door opened.

I stepped off the platform and away from the trap door. Spidox then retracted the webbing back into her uncovering the opening.

"Are those steps?" Jax asked.

"They are. I wonder where they lead," Mylo said.

Jax knelt down and noticed that they lead back towards the wall. "Well, that's strange. Why not just open a door in the wall? Why do we have

Chapter 3 Inside The Castle Walls

to go down the steps just to come back to where the wall is?"

"Maybe they lead to another door," Kennz said.

"Yeah, and then another...and another. Who knows where they go? It could lead to a dead end or just put us on a wild goose chase. Again, you can't see past the wall since it's dark. Unless we have light we won't be able to see down there either," explained Jax.

"Uh, guys...we need to pick one or the other real quick," yelled Spidox. "We have visitors coming."

My horn somehow made an appearance and dropped to the ground. Everyone looked at it in amazement. I quickly picked it up and it illuminated.

"Where did that come from and can you now transform?" asked Jax.

"No time to find out. Everyone down the steps," I directed.

We quickly went down the trap door and I pointed my horn towards the symbol on the wall. A beam of light came shooting out of it hitting the symbol causing the door to close protecting us from the oncoming herd of snoads.

"Quick thinking, Nia," said Allie.

"Thanks. I think we'll be heading this way instead of the corridor."

"Why did your horn just appear?" Allie asked.

"No idea. Maybe it has something to do with me touching the symbol. It's weird, though, because it fell off of my head, but at least we can see where we're going now."

Chapter 3 Inside The Castle Walls

Just like Jax said the stair led right back to the wall and stopped.

"This makes no sense. Why would they just stop here?" Jax asked.

"Maybe this was a secret hideout for the snoads in case they were attacked," Mylo answered.

"Mylo, the snoads wouldn't be able to activate the symbol, so I don't think so," said Margot.

"She's right, Mylo, but these stairs were put here for a reason. Let me illuminate the area a little more. Again, if anyone sees anything…" I was saying when the others interrupted.

"…yell out that we've found something. We know," the others said, then laughing since they all said it at the same time.

I illuminated the area more brightly and in unison the others pointed straight ahead and yelled out, "Found it!"

A door appeared the more the area was illuminated. "I think we have our answer." I then pushed on the door and it opened right away.

We walked through it and it closed immediately upon the last one walking past it.

"Where are we?" asked Kennz.

"It looks like we are inside the castle walls," answered Mylo.

"Now what, Nia?" Kennz asked.

"It looks like we need to find our way through since I don't think the door is going to open up behind us. It feels like the only control I have over this horn, right now anyway, is to make it glow brighter or dim it when I need it to."

Chapter 3 Inside The Castle Walls

"How bright can you get that to glow, Nia?" Jax asked.

"Not sure. I've never had to test that out."

"I think this would be a good time to do that," he said.

I didn't think it could hurt anything so I closed my eyes and held the horn out in front of me and focused on making it glow as bright as possible. The brighter it glowed the more things around us started to disappear.

"Nia, you might want to pull back on the glowy stick right now," Margot cautiously said.

I opened up my eyes and saw things in front of us disappearing.

I tried dialing it down but it kept increasing the glow power.

"Nia...make it stop!" yelled Jax.

"I'm trying. It's not listening to me."

"Let go of it. That should stop it," he then told me.

I let go of it but it didn't drop. It hovered right where it was and continued to glow even brighter...until it just stopped.

"Whoa! How'd it do that?" Mylo asked.

"More importantly, what is that over there?" Allie asked, pointing straight ahead.

"It can't be!" I exclaimed.

"It can't be what?" asked Jax.

"This is the spot Legend took me inside the cave when I had to freeze you all in time. This is where one of the SWOOZLs was hidden," I said grabbing my horn out of mid-air.

We walked towards the rocks that were now in front of us when we saw one of them glowing.

"Could that be what I think it is?" Allie asked.

Chapter 3 Inside The Castle Walls

"If you're thinking a scroll, more importantly one that appears to be glowing a golden color inside that rock, then yes, we're thinking the same thing," I answered.

"How do we get it out of there?" Mylo asked.

"My horn has done most of the work up til now. I used it the last time I was in here to gain control of the SWOOZL, so let's see if I can use it to gain control of the scroll."

I held my horn in one hand and reached my other toward the glowing rock. I felt the outside of it and a strange force enveloped my body. I then pushed on the rock until I felt my hand going through it. My hand was fully immersed into the stone when I felt the scroll. I looked up at the others and had a huge smile on my face.

"I think she's retrieved the first scroll," Margot said.

"Maybe it's just a glow bug and it's tickling her hand," Jax quipped.

"That's a big bug to be glowing like that. I don't think I would be laughing unless I knew it was friendly," Kennz said.

The others looked at her and shook their heads. I began to laugh a little while not losing my concentration on getting the scroll out.

I wrapped my fingers around the parchment and slowly pulled it out of the rock. I kept a slow pace not wanting to damage it in anyway. When it was completely out from the rock I let out a deep breath.

"That was pretty cool," Allie said. "Should we open it up and see what is on there?"

Chapter 3 Inside The Castle Walls

"Not now." I then turned to Margot and handed the scroll over to her.

"Why are you giving this to me?" she asked.

"Like Jax said...your tree," I told her.

"What am I supposed to do with it?"

"Hide it. Use your talismans and absorb it for now. When the time is right we'll put them all together and see what they tell us. I don't think that each of them are going to make any sense by themselves. I think it's just like what happened with our folders back in the Archive Room. We need to get them all together before we can make sense of them."

Margot summoned her talismans and made them become one on her forehead. She then held the scroll up to it. Her talisman began to glow and absorbed the energy of the scroll. The scroll then vanished from her hand while the talisman sunk back into her forehead.

"Now what?" asked Allie.

"I think we need to find King Olly and have a talk with him. Maybe he can tell us more about the morpions. Plus, when I had my hand on the scroll I was able to absorb more information."

"Like what?" Jax asked.

"Let's find the king. I think the questions I have for him will make more sense hearing his answers instead of coming from me. Let's get out of here and head back up."

Before we left the room Kennz stopped and looked back towards the rocks.

"What is it, Kennz?" Margot asked her.

"What about the glowing bug? Are we just going to leave it there?"

Chapter 3 Inside The Castle Walls

"Kennz, let's go!" Margot exclaimed, grabbing a hold of her arm and pulling her along.

While we were walking Mylo put his arm around Kennz and asked her, "You do realize there is no glowy bug inside that rock, right?"

"Not anymore. When Nia took the scroll out the bug stopped glowing," she said.

"Really, Kennz?" Margot remarked.

"Let's just get going and find King Olly," I told them while shaking my head and chuckling.

Chapter 4 Understanding the Past

We quickly but quietly made our way back up to the trap door. Before opening it up, I took my horn and illuminated it a little while slightly opening the door. I peeked out but did not notice any of the snoads around. Jax and Mylo were feeling brave and decided to force the door open quickly and then jumped out striking the fiercest poses they could come up with. They were back to back to each other and then turned 360 degrees looking to see if they could find any of the snoads. The four of us saw what they were doing and started to laugh.

Chapter 4 Understanding the Past

"You two look a little like *'Charlie's Angels'*, just not the Angels part," I told them.

"Yeah! What's with the faces? Do you guys think you look intimidating or something?" asked Margot.

"We're protecting you all since we can't change into our forms," Mylo told her.

Margot then stepped out from the trap door and turned into Spidox. "I think I can take on whomever without your help," she told them, flicking a web their way before changing back.

"We were just trying to help," Jax said, a bit disgruntled, pulling the webbing off of him.

"Well I found it charming," I said, smiling at Jax walking up to him and picking the last piece of webbing from him.

"Shh!" Allie said to us, while putting her finger up to her lips.

"What do you hear?" I whispered to Allie.

She put her head forward and turned it slightly. "Nothing. I'm not hearing anything."

"Then why did you shush us?" Kennz asked.

"Don't you guys find it a little strange that there are no snoads around here...anywhere? How many were chasing us? I would have figured that we would have been met by at least a couple of them waiting for our return," replied Allie.

I looked around and thought it was rather weird how silent it was.

"You're right, Allie. It is a little odd that none of the snoads are around here," I said.

Margot then quickly changed into Spidox and flung herself around shooting a few webs and trapping something.

Chapter 4 Understanding the Past

"You can release me, Margot," the voice mumbled from under the webbing.

Margot quickly changed back and ran up to the person. She put her hands on the webbing and immediately absorbed it back into herself.

"Dad? Is it really you?" Margot asked.

"It is and you pack a nice little punch with your webs. I'm impressed," he told her.

"But what happened to you? Are you still a snoad and how do you know who I am now? You're not young any longer. I'm confused." she told him.

"I know you are," he said to her and then looked at the rest of us. "I'm sure you all are. Let's get out of here before the rest of the castle disappears."

"Disappears? What do you mean? How does a castle just disappear?" I asked, not believing him.

He didn't answer my question directly, instead saying, "Quick! Follow me and we'll get out of here." He walked towards the gate to the dungeon and opened it up.

"How did you do that? The key is still under my webbing over there," Margot said, pointing at the floor on the other side.

Margot's father, Oliver, didn't answer and instead walked towards the back wall of the dungeon and pushed on a few of the cobblestones. The wall opened up. "You might want to hurry so none of you disappear," he said pointing behind us.

We were in awe of what was happening seeing the entire castle vanishing right before our

Chapter 4 Understanding the Past

eyes, but quickly ran out so the void didn't trap us while it was swallowing the castle.

We got outside just in time to watch the last of the castle disappear.

"Can you tell us what is going on?" Margot asked him.

"Let's get back to the door leading out from your tree and I will help to explain what is happening," he replied.

"I'm not even going to ask how you know that we are inside my tree," she responded.

We got back on the path and followed it towards the door of the tree. Margot went up to the door and tried to push it open but it wouldn't budge.

"It's locked from the other side," Oliver yelled out.

"Then how are we supposed to get out of here and how do you know that?" Margot quizzically asked him.

"However you all got into the tree is how you should leave it," he said. He then looked at me motioning for me to go to the door.

"What do you want me to do? I used my staff to get us in here. I have my horn but can't summon my staff," I told him.

"Look at your arm," he told me.

I looked down and saw that it was glowing a blueish-white color.

"How?" I asked dumbfounded. "Whatever!" I exclaimed, walking towards the door. I stretched my arm out and was able to summon my staff. I then held it up towards the door and it immediately opened up. We walked out and were once again in the midst of the six trees.

Chapter 4 Understanding the Past

We looked back at Margot's tree and noticed the door had disappeared. Her tree now glowed a really bright purple, which was now glowing brighter than the other trees.

"Okay...what is going on? Why did you send the snoads to look for Spidox when you knew that she would never be found since Margot was with us?" I asked him.

"Wait a minute? You knew who I was and who we were all this time?" Margot asked. "Why didn't you tell us earlier? Why were you so young when we first saw you? Why were you able to turn into a snoad and then tell us that you had no idea who War Fox was? What happened to all of the snoads? Why did the door to my tree disappear? Can we get it back?"

He looked at Margot and she raised her hands slightly gesturing towards him waiting for him to answer.

"I wasn't sure if you were done with all of the questions or not," he said, laughing a little. "If you are, then I am ready to answer them."

"For right now, yes I am. I'm sure I can think of more, but I will wait," Margot kindly said to him.

He found a big enough rock to sit on. He then said, "You all might want to find something comfortable to sit on as well. We may be a here for a little bit."

Each of us found a rock or stump or even a comfy spot on the ground to sit on. I looked at the others and then back towards Oliver. "I think we are comfy and ready."

Chapter 4 Understanding the Past

"Okay. As for the last question you asked about the tree...every time you obtain a scroll and exit the tree it will do that, thus preventing you from ever being able to go back in there again."

"We'll never be able to go back into our own trees?" Allie asked.

"Not after you obtain the scroll from it." He then paused before answering again. "I guess it could be possible, but only if Nia allows it. She would have to hide or put something in there and then reopen it. I don't see why she would have to do that once all of the scrolls are found. I don't know of anything else she would have to hide." He then turned to me and asked, "Do you?"

"I didn't even know I hid each of the scrolls in the trees until a short time ago, so, as of right now, I have no idea how to answer that. Before you get to the other questions, when were we? We all think that was Forest Creek, but just not sure when it was."

"You are right with both of those assumptions and I will add more to that. That was definitely Forest Creek, just a while ago. And, yes, that was me back then, King of the Snoads. I knew who you all were when I saw you. I just couldn't let the snoads know."

"Why?" I curiously asked.

"Because then you wouldn't have found what you came here looking for. I had to make sure and give you all a nudge. I also had to make sure the snoads were distracted looking for Spidox knowing that they would never find her."

"I have a few questions," Jax said, raising his hand.

"What is it, Jax?" Oliver asked.

Chapter 4 Understanding the Past

"When did you become the War Fox? Why not be the War Snoad or something like that?" Jax asked him.

"Great questions and a tough question for me to answer," he told him.

"Why's that?" asked Jax.

Oliver hesitated for a few seconds and then sighed before answering. "Because, Jax, I feel like I let my people down."

"Are you referring to the snoads, dad?" Margot asked.

"I am, kiddo," Oliver said, a bit dejected. "You see, after the Grand Mermaid found the five of us, she asked us to come here. She said this land was mythical and full of fantasy. Naturally, we were all curious and had to see it for ourselves. We were all assigned a role. The Grand Mermaid convinced other creatures to come back to the

Whispering Pines Forest and make it their home along with the mermaids and morpions that were still here. She promised that they would be protected. I was tasked with being the leader of the snoads and some of the other creatures of the land. Unfortunately, the remaining morpion figured out how to run the snoads out of the forest."

"Did the morpion run all of the creatures out of the land?" Kennz asked.

"He did not. Not that he didn't try. The Grand Mermaid asked Ms. Z, or General Z as she was known, to take me under her wing and show me how to be a great fighter and protector of this land. I didn't realize it at the time, but this is when Z came back and asked to not have anything to do with the land. The Grand Mermaid asked for one more favor. That happened to be helping me become the War Fox and then take her place, before

Chapter 4 Understanding the Past

she officially stepped down." He then paused and looked at us asking, "Any other questions?"

Mylo raised his hand and asked, "What were those statues made of back in the castle?"

"The statues? Was there something wrong with them?" Oliver asked Mylo.

"No. It's just that they felt weird. They were mushy like," said Mylo.

"Oh, I know what you are talking about. They are made of different materials, but mostly from bojo berries," he answered.

"Bojo berries? Those sound familiar. Why them?" I curiously asked.

"Snoads are known for planting and harvesting bojo berries. They showed the pixlets the benefits of them before departing Forest Creek. The pixlets and the guardian fairies now plant them all over the area. They are used for many things, but also have a healing power to them."

"What type of healing power?" asked Kennz.

"A healing power that saved your father, Kennz," he told her.

"Is that the plant my father found that helped heal Kennz's dad, Zenith?" asked Jax.

"That is the one. Although, at the time, they were very scarce. If I remember correctly, the other Originals were out on an expedition when Zenith fell ill. Jax's father vowed to protect him and find the one thing that could heal him. It's not the berries, themselves, that have the healing ability; instead, he had to get the liquid from the stalk of the plant and give it to Zenith to save him."

"Is that when he gave my dad the jackalope foot or whatever it was?" Jax asked him.

Chapter 4 Understanding the Past

"It was. Your dad didn't know what to do with it right away and asked for advice from us after they returned. He figured it was one of Zenith's artifacts and wanted to return it back to him. Zenith wouldn't allow him to and simply told him that he would know what to do with it one day. That's how you got hold of it."

"I have a question," I began. "Z told us that the snoads are water creatures. Why wasn't the castle surrounded by water or, at least, near water? That doesn't make sense to me."

Oliver looked at me and was contemplating how to answer the question. After a few seconds he finally answered. "You are right, Nia, about the snoads being water creatures. That's how the morpion originally was able to run them out. He figured out how to drain them of their main resource. The snoads kept a lot of the bojo berries in the waters around here and when the water was just about gone is when they left. The Grand Mermaid tried to convince them to come back to the land. She promised that they would have an abundance of water supplied to them but they haven't returned, yet. I hear that you have found the lake," he then said.

"We found the hidden falls and lake. That's where I found the last piece of the SWOOZL," I told him. After a quick pause I asked, "We found the first of the golden scrolls where one of the pieces to the SWOOZL was located. Is that where each tree will take us, where each piece of the SWOOZLs were found?"

"I believe that is how you set it up. But I do have to warn you, the encounter you had with me will not be the same with the others. When you are

Chapter 4 Understanding the Past

in the other trees the other Originals may not treat you as kindly as I have. Just be prepared."

"Why is that? Why would the Originals be in our trees? Why were you in Margot's?" Jax asked him.

"That's how the Grand Mermaid set it up. These trees were originally ours. She didn't want to make it easy for anyone to be able to obtain the scrolls. She set it up so each Original was the guardian of one of the scrolls. Her intention was to have the Original of that tree to be its guardian and the protector of the scroll."

"Why were you so easy on us then?" Margot asked him.

"Since I was the first tree and the first scroll to be found, I was allowed to take it easy on you all. Again, that won't always be the case."

Allie sat there with a really confused look on her face which I had noticed.

"What's wrong, Allie?" I asked her.

She looked at Oliver and asked, "Who's going to be the Original guarding my tree since I'm not a descendant of an Original?"

Oliver looked directly at me and then pointed my direction.

"Wait a minute...you're saying that we will have to fight me for a scroll?" I tensely asked.

"I didn't say that, but it will either be you or Wesam. Look, don't take it out on me. You set all of this up...well, the Grand Mermaid, but there's more," he began.

"Oh great! I can't wait to hear this," I proclaimed. "What is it?"

"I'm afraid someone else will be there, too," he said.

Chapter 4 Understanding the Past

"Who else will be in there?" Allie asked.

"Do you have all of the pieces to the SWOOZL, Nia?" Oliver asked.

"I have all but one. The morpion has the other," I stated.

"Then you will also have to battle the morpion. He probably will not be alone, either," Oliver told us.

"That means my dad will more than likely be in there, too," said Allie. "And the other lady that is with them."

"More than likely," Oliver told her.

We sat there in silence for a few moments contemplating what had been told to us before Allie spoke up. "If it means we have to fight my dad for the scroll then we'll have to do it."

"Will you be okay doing that?" Jax asked her.

"It sounds like we will have to fight each of your parents to get a scroll, so what's the difference?" she answered.

"I guess you're right, but it seems like it will be different since we will have to take on more than just Nia...or, I mean, the Grand Mermaid, in some manner," Jax told her. "I say that we get moving on to the next tree and scroll. Anything else you can tell us or advice you can give us?" Jax asked, looking at Oliver.

"Up 'til the last tree it will only be you six that can obtain the scroll," he answered.

"What makes the last scroll different?" I asked him.

"That's all I can say besides stick together, have each others' backs, and good luck. We're all counting on you." After saying that Oliver quickly vanished right in front of us.

Chapter 4 Understanding the Past

"Um...where did your dad just disappear to, Margot?" Kennz asked.

"No idea. That was weird," Margot remarked, tilting her head back and forth and then looking around. She then began speaking again, "I second what Jax said. We should get moving on to the next tree and see what we are faced with."

"Before we do that I have one request," Mylo said.

"What's that?" Margot asked him.

"Can we eat? I'm hungry."

"When are you not?!" Margot said to him.

Chapter 5 The Magic Words

We stood up and walked to the center of the trees looking around to see which one would allow us to enter it. The locks were still on the doors but nothing was happening.

"Well this is fun just waiting!" exclaimed Margot.

"Isn't something supposed to happen like it did with Margot's tree?" Allie asked.

"I thought it would, but I'm not sure," I told her.

"Maybe we need to go up to the door and ask it politely if we can come in," Kennz told us.

Chapter 5 The Magic Words

Jax looked at her and laughed. "You know what, Kennz, I think you're right. You should go up to your door and politely ask if we can come in," he told her sarcastically shaking his head at her while still laughing.

Kennz thought nothing of Jax's snide comment and promptly walked over to her tree and knelt down in front of the door. "Can you let us in please?" she asked.

Just then the lock on the door released its grip and fell off. Kennz pushed on the door and then immediately transformed into her Glipin form and whisked into her tree.

Jax's jaw dropped and was dumbfounded at what just happened.

"She's not a ditz all the time," Mylo told him, walking by patting him on his back.

Jax didn't know how to respond and mumbled under his breath, "I guess not."

"Let's remember how we got in. Kennz will have to apparently ask the door if it can let us out. We just need to make sure she is nice about it," I remarked.

The five of us went into her tree. Upon entering, the door quickly shut behind us. We then spotted Glipin gliding in the air while the cool breeze gently brushed her whiskers back into her face as if she didn't have a care in the world. We watched as she glided and swooped through the air going in and out of the trees.

"Hey, wait a minute! These are our trees!" exclaimed Jax. "Nia, you found a piece of the SWOOZL at the top of your tree. This must be where the next scroll is."

Chapter 5 The Magic Words

I looked around, but something didn't seem right with me. "It can't be this easy," I told the others. "Oliver said that getting the other scrolls would become increasingly more difficult. This doesn't seem right."

"Maybe he didn't know about this tree," Allie said.

"I don't know, Allie. Something seems off," I told her.

We continued to look around until Mylo blurted out, "Has anyone seen Glipin?"

"She was just up…" I started to say when I couldn't spot her any longer. "Where did she go? I don't like this," I stated walking around trying to find her.

We spread out and started yelling for Glipin and Kennz not knowing which form she might be in, but never hearing anything in return from her.

We gathered back at the trees wondering what happened to Glipin.

"What are we going to do?" Allie asked.

"I don't know. We need to find her. I just don't think Glipin would have flown off on her own without us seeing her. She was right up there," I said pointing up towards the tops of the trees. I then curiously looked at the top of my tree and walked a little closer to it.

"What is it, Nia?" Margot asked.

"I think I see something up there, but I can't seem to make it out," I told her.

Mylo looked up and then shouted, "It's her! It's Glipin!" He quickly ran to my tree and started to shake it trying to cause her to fall from the top. He used all his might since he couldn't transform and was finally able to shake her loose. She fell, tumbling through the branches with Mylo keeping

Chapter 5 The Magic Words

a keen eye on her. He followed her movement through the branches until she approached the ground. He flung his arms out and caught her right before she was going to hit the ground. Mylo stared at her for a few seconds and then brought Glipin over to us.

"She's not looking to well," Jax observed.

Margot looked over at my tree and noticed something about it. "Nia, your tree looks like it is wilting away."

I turned and saw the color disappear from it and started to droop. "Something's wrong with my tree. We need to bring it back to life!" I exclaimed.

"Excuse me?!" Mylo yelled. "We need to save Glipin. No disrespect to you or your tree, but we're talking about Glipin here. I need her back. I need Kennz back," he said, close to tearing up.

Allie went over and consoled Mylo. "Nia, she's not looking well. I agree with Mylo. We need to focus on Glipin and make her well again."

I looked at the both of them and tried to muster up the courage for what I was about to say. "I think you're both wrong," I said, now turning and looking at my tree. "I think if we can bring my tree back to life it will somehow someway make Glipin well again."

"How do you propose we do that?" asked Margot.

I then turned and looked at Jax. "What?" he asked. "How am I supposed to know how to make her better?"

I walked over to him and put my hand on his shoulder. "Think about what is happening and it will come to you," I told him.

Chapter 5 The Magic Words

Jax then pulled away and walked towards my tree and looked at it. He then walked over to Glipin and saw how her condition was deteriorating. "I don't know what you want me to do! I can't transform and I certainly don't have a magical potion to fix this," he was saying before it dawned on him. He then had a smile on his face. "Mylo, she's going to be fine. I need to go find something."

"Find what?" Mylo asked him.

"The same thing that healed her father...the stalk of a bojo berry."

"Where are you going to find one of those?" Allie asked him.

"There's got to be some around here. Nia, didn't you say that the pixlets and guardian fairies plant them?" asked Jax.

"They do," I said, trying to remember where I saw them planting them. "Got it! Over by the creek. That is where I saw them. I'll go with you," I told him. I then turned and looked at the others. "Stay here with her and take care of her. We'll be back soon." I then turned my attention to Mylo. "She's going to be okay. I'll make sure of it." Jax and I then quickly ran towards the creek.

"This would be so much faster and easier if we could transform," Jax yelled out while we were running.

"It would be, but we can't. Let's just hope that we can find some in time."

"But I thought you told Mylo that she was going to be okay. Is that not true?"

"She's not looking well, Jax. I don't know how much time we really have. I'm just holding on hope to the story of how your father saved Zenith.

Chapter 5 The Magic Words

He believed and didn't give up. We need to do the same, just quickly."

We ran to the place where I remembered seeing the pixlets and guardian fairies planting the berries. It quickly turned cold and gray.

"What is happening?" Jax asked.

Before I could answer I saw a pixlet, but it seemed colorless and was moving about slowly albeit looking lifeless. We quickly ran up to it. Its eyes seemed lifeless and was gazing forward without nowhere in particular to go. I did notice that it had something in it's hand. It looked like a bojo berry.

"Can you give us the berry? We need it to save our friends life," I said to the pixlet.

The pixlet stopped for a second but then continued to walk again staring forward.

"We need to get that berry. What should we do?" Jax asked.

I thought for a few seconds and then said, "I've got it. How did Kennz get us into her tree?" I caught up with the pixlet again, but this time asked nicely, "Can you give us the bojo berry, please? We need it to save our friends life."

The pixlet stopped and turned to me holding the berry out in front of him. I put my hand out and he dropped it in my hand, only to see it quickly ooze through my fingers and fall to the ground. The pixlet then turned and continued to walk aimlessly away from us.

"Now what, Jax? We need to find the berries or the plants. I just don't think we are going to find them here."

Jax then had a look on his face and told me to follow him.

Chapter 5 The Magic Words

"Where are we going?" I asked him.

"Back to the others," he answered.

"We don't have anything that is going to help."

"Not yet. Just trust me."

We both sprinted as expeditiously as we could to get to the others. We finally spotted them sitting among the trees comforting Glipin.

Margot noticed us running back and quickly sprang to her feet. "Did you find it?" she eagerly asked.

"We did, but can't use it," I told her.

Mylo heard what I said. By now he was on the verge of tears when he asked me, "I thought you said she was going to be fine. How are you going to heal her?"

"Bro, she'll be fine!" Jax exclaimed.

I was getting a little worried and didn't know what Jax had planned. "Jax, we're running out of time. What are you going to do?" I asked him.

He looked back at me and then at Margot. "We need to get back into Margot's tree," he said.

"We can't. You heard my dad. Once we leave we can't get back in unless Nia hides something in there. Plus, without Kennz, we're not getting out of this tree," Margot replied.

"You're right, but I don't want to leave this tree. I just want to get into that one," he said pointing at Margot's tree.

"Even if we can get in there, what makes you think we are going to find what we need?" I asked.

"Remember what Oliver told us?"

Chapter 5 The Magic Words

Margot and I looked at each other and shrugged our shoulders. "What, Jax? He said a lot of things to us. Where are you going with this?" I asked.

"He said it was the snoads that showed the pixlets how to plant the bojo berries. I bet anything we will find some back in there."

"It's worth a shot," I told him. I then looked at Margot. "Can you get us into your tree? I can't summon anything right now."

Margot ran over to her tree and looked it over. She then placed her hands on the tree. Upon doing so, her other pedipalps appeared. Her tree then glowed a purple color and a door appeared. Margot then turned to Jax and I. "What are we waiting for? Let's go get that plant."

Jax and I followed Margot into her tree. The door didn't shut behind us like last time, but we knew we needed to hurry.

"Where should we go to find what we need?" Margot asked.

Jax and I blurted out at the same time, "The creek."

The three of us quickly ran until we spotted someone standing by the creek. When we got closer we could see that it was a man holding a bucket in one hand while picking berries from a plant with his other. We ran up to him to get his attention. He turned to us and we recognized him, but he had that same gaze in his eyes that the pixlet had.

"Zenith?" I asked.

It was definitely Kennz's father, just not as lively. In a loud and harsh voice he screamed at us

Chapter 5 The Magic Words

asking "What do you want?" He then went back to picking the berries and putting them in the bucket.

Jax ran in front of him to get his attention. "Sir, we need to borrow a few of the stalks of your bojo berry plants. We need to save your daughter," he told him.

"These are mine. Go away!" he demanded and then continued to walk picking more berries.

"Maybe we should just grab a few of the stalks and run back," Margot suggested.

"Not a bad idea," Jax said as he went to grab a few of the stalks.

Just then Zenith heard what was happening and turned around quickly moving towards Jax, now standing in front of him.

"I said go away. Leave my plants alone." He then pushed on Jax forcing him to fall to the ground. Zenith then turned and started picking more berries.

Jax quickly jumped back to his feet and composed himself.

"Jax, I don't think we should mess with him any longer. We need to get out of here and find another way of saving Glipin," I told him.

"We don't have time. He has what we need. We just need to figure out how to get it."

Margot then blurted out, "Why don't we take Kennz's approach and just ask nicely?"

Jax looked at me and I at Margot. "It's worth a shot," Jax replied.

Jax quickly got in front of Zenith and stopped him one more time. "Sir, we are in need of a few of these stalks. Our friend will not survive without them. May we please take a couple of them so we can save her life?"

Chapter 5 The Magic Words

Zenith's eyes then changed and there was life in them. He turned and saw Margot and I standing there.

"Is my baby girl alright?" he asked.

"She won't be if we don't get a few of these back to her quickly," I told him.

His eyes began to well up and a few tears dripped from them. He turned and yanked a few of the stalks out of the ground. He then turned and handed them to Jax. "Your father saved my life because he believed and wouldn't give up on me. Thank you for not giving up on my daughter."

Jax looked at him and told him, "It's what my father would expect of me to do." Jax then turned and looked at us, "Let's get hurrying. We don't have much time."

We quickly sprinted back to the door of Margot's tree. We could see the door was starting to close on its own. "Why can't this be easy?" I yelled out. "Let's hurry!"

Margot got there first and quickly got through. Jax then gave me a nudge to follow her. Margot and I were safely out of the tree anxiously awaiting for Jax to come through. The door was getting very close to fully being closed. In the nick of time Jax come flopping through as he somewhat dove avoiding the door.

"Well it wasn't graceful, but it worked," I said, smiling at him helping him up.

The others saw us. Allie yelled out, "Did you get it?"

"We did," Jax responded.

We quickly ran over to them. Jax broke the stalk of one of the plants and handed it to Mylo. Mylo grabbed it and was about to pour it into

Chapter 5 The Magic Words

Glipin's mouth. He stopped and looked at me and then handed me the stalk. "I trust you."

I took the stalk from his hand and quickly ran to my tree. I knelt down and poured the juice out of the stalk towards the basin of the tree. My tree began to show a resemblance of life, but not that much. I turned to the others to check to see what was happening with Glipin. She still looked lifeless in Mylo's arms. Mylo looked at me, but I could still see in his eyes that he trusted me.

"Jax, bring me another stalk, please," I yelled to him.

Jax ran over to me and had already snapped the stalk for me before reaching me. He handed it to me and I knelt down again. This time I noticed an acorn lying on the ground. I grabbed it with my other hand. I looked at the stalk and then the acorn. I put both of them on the ground and quickly dug a hole next to the tree. I put the acorn in the hole and then covered it up. I took the stalk and held it over the newly covered hole squeezing out as much of the juice from it I could. The juice was rapidly absorbed by the earth. After a few seconds the ground around us started to quake.

    Jax and I quickly stepped away. I looked down and could see a glow coming from where I buried the acorn. The glow latched onto the tree and instantly rose to the top of it, glowing brightly. Jax and I turned to the others to see if they were seeing what we were. The others were looking at what we were when Mylo fell backwards and was no longer holding onto Glipin. The glow from the top of my tree shot towards Glipin causing her to spring up and do a somersault. She glided up towards the top of my tree where the glow was originating from. She was there only a few seconds

Chapter 5 The Magic Words

when she swooped down towards us stopping right in front of me with her arms held out holding onto something. I put my hands out. She then dropped the scroll with me catching it. Glipin then transformed back into Kennz.

"Are you okay?" I asked her.

"What happened?" she asked.

Mylo quickly ran over to her giving her a kiss and hugging her. "Don't you remember anything?" he asked.

Kennz stared at him shaking her head. "The last thing I remember is asking the door if we could come in. And now I am standing in front of Nia."

"You don't remember turning into Glipin and flying around inside of here?" I asked.

"Nope. I'm not even sure how I got in here," Kennz replied. "Did you find the scroll?" she asked.

I looked at Margot and Jax and then back at Kennz, "If it wasn't for you we wouldn't have," I told her, chuckling a little.

"I don't understand," she replied.

"Don't worry about it," I told her and then gave her a hug. I let go of her and walked over to my tree and unearthed the acorn I buried. I then walked over to Kennz and handed it to her.

"This is just like the acorn you and I were playing with when we were up here," she said.

"Do me a favor and use it to absorb this scroll and then absorb it into your body," I told her.

Kennz knelt down and placed the acorn on the ground under one of her hands and the scroll under her other. She then absorbed them: the scroll into the acorn and the acorn into her body.

Chapter 5 The Magic Words

"Nicely done," I told her. I then looked at the others and said, "Let's get out of here, but let's be polite when we leave."

Kennz walked to the door and, again, asked it if we could leave. The door opened up and we all left her tree. Kennz was the last to leave and whispered something to the door right before it disappeared. She then walked over to where we were.

"What did you say to it?" I asked her.

"I told it 'Thank You'!"

That's Kennz for you.

Chapter 6 KENNZ'S VISION

We stood, again, in the center of the trees.

"Which one do you think will be next?" Allie asked.

"Not sure," I told her and then looked at the others. "I don't think we should be so quick to enter into the next one," I said.

"Why's that, Nia?" asked Margot.

"I think we should talk about what we've seen and what might be left," I was telling them when I noticed Mylo was about to speak and then I began again before he could say anything. "I also think we should get something to eat."

Mylo looked at me and put his fist out for a fist bump. "I'm all in for that," he told me.

Chapter 6 Kennz's Vision

"I think we are all a bit hungry," Allie told him. "I know that I am."

Everyone nodded their head yes. It took about fifteen minutes to get back to the RV. No one said a word on the way there. I think we were all trying to gather ourselves and prepare for what might happen in the other four trees.

It was nice to see the RV again. It seemed like we had been away from it for quite some time. I know we all needed to just rest, relax, and reset our minds. Once we got to the RV, we made a few sandwiches, grabbed some chips and water, and then sat at the table to eat. No one said anything while we ate. We each had one sandwich, except for Mylo, he had three...and still finished before the rest of us. After eating we cleaned up and then spread out in the RV to give each of us some room. I stayed at the table.

"So, what do we know so far about the first two trees?" I asked the group.

"We know that we've already been in Margot's and Kennz's and that leaves mine, Jax's, Mylo's, and yours," Allie started.

"We also know that we will be getting the scrolls from the same place where the pieces of the SWOOZLs were recovered," continued Margot.

"Except for the last one," Jax said. "Nia, have you been able to remember when and where the morpion was able to obtain the final piece of the SWOOZL?'

"I wish I could remember. I've been trying ever since I told everyone back in my basement."

"What about the form you gave him? We know he is originally a morpion, but you said you gave him a form or ability. Do you remember what it was?" asked Margot.

Chapter 6 Kennz's Vision

I sat back on the bench seat and thought for a few moments.

"Guys, I wish I could. I still don't remember everything, yet. I know it's got to be frustrating for you guys, but how do you think I feel?"

"None of us would want to be you right now, Nia. We're just hoping that you can remember the important stuff when it matters most," Margot said.

"Me, too, Margot. Me, too," I told her.

"Let's get back to the scrolls," Jax chimed in with. "We have already faced Kennz and Margot's dads. That still leaves my dad, Mylo's mom, I'm assuming Wesam, and then you in some sort of form, Nia. Am I correct?"

"I think you're correct, Jax," I told him. "I just don't know how I am going to present myself."

I then paused for a few moments and then began again, "I'm telling you right now, no matter what happens, make sure you get the scroll from my tree if I am bad or evil or anything like that, because, at this point, nothing would surprise me."

"Do you really think you would do that to yourself?" Allie asked.

"What do you mean?" I asked her.

"Do you really think you would have put something like this together knowing that you would have to battle yourself and make it difficult on you? I'm thinking that you did this so no one else could get the scrolls," Allie replied.

"We already know that is exactly why she did this – to make sure that no one but her could get them. Not sure what you mean by your statement, Allie," Jax told her.

Chapter 6 Kennz's Vision

"Don't you get it, Jax? Maybe we're approaching this all wrong. Maybe we need to take a cue from Kennz and simply ask for the scrolls; especially if they know it is Nia who is trying to obtain them," responded Allie.

"That didn't work with Kennz's tree, Allie," Margot said. "It was almost a little puzzle we had to solve. Based upon what happened in my tree, we had to use a clue from that to figure out how to get the scroll from Kennz's. Each tree may be building off the previous one. I don't think we'll really know until we get to that tree."

"I think you're right about not knowing until we get into the tree, Margot," I began. "But I don't believe that each tree will build on what happened in the previous. I think that was just more of a coincidence than anything."

"What makes you believe that?" Kennz asked.

"In your tree, Kennz, yes, we did have to figure out to go back to Margot's tree for the bojo berries, but it was mostly Jax that had to do that."

"Still not following," Kennz replied.

"I would have figured that Jax's tree would have been second if they were really connected. It was Jax's father that saved your father. I would have figured we would have been taken into Jax's tree before yours."

"Good point, Nia. Any guesses who's tree will be next?" Allie asked.

Everyone looked around the RV at the four who were left. I looked at Kennz and asked, "Kennz, whose next?"

Kennz didn't hesitate and said, "Mylo's. I believe Mylo's will be next."

Chapter 6 Kennz's Vision

Mylo looked at her strangely. "Mine? Why do you think that?"

"Just a hunch," she said.

"What? Did you ask your tree or something?" Jax asked in jest.

"No. I didn't need to. I just feel it," she answered.

We looked at her somewhat suspicious of the statement she just made. "What do you mean you just 'feel it'? Did something happen in your tree that you've not told us?" I asked her.

"Yeah! You said you couldn't remember anything. Was that a lie?" Jax yelled out.

"Honestly, I don't remember much inside of my tree. I'm not quite sure why I think Mylo's will be next. I think I was shown it."

"Shown it? Are you sure you just didn't ask nicely whose tree was next?" Again, Jax asked a bit snarky.

"Jax, enough will you!" I told him. I then asked Kennz to come sit over with me at the table. Kennz came over and sat across from me.

"What is it, Nia?" she asked me.

I looked at Margot and without even having to ask she said, "You need my eyes, don't you?"

"I do. Do you mind coming over here, please?" I asked her.

I scooted over a little so Margot could sit next to me. The other three gathered around the table to see what I was up to. I placed my horn in front of Kennz's forehead. She moved her head slightly to the side of it and looked at me.

"Don't worry. This won't hurt at all. At least, I don't think," I said, giving her a little wink.

Chapter 6 Kennz's Vision

I took a deep breath and then focused my energy at the horn. "Margot, please summon your talismans into a single one and then look at the horn."

Margot didn't have to turn full on Spidox to summon her talismans and have them combine as one in the middle of her forehead. Once they did that I took control of them as they turned blue and focused more on the horn.

Energy and light emitted from the horn going to Kennz's forehead. I concentrated on what it had shown Kennz while she was in her tree. I then let go of the control and Margot turned back to herself. I absorbed my horn back into me.

"What did you see?" Allie asked.

"Well, Kennz is right. Mylo's tree is next," I told her.

"Did it show you what will happen in my tree?" Mylo asked.

"It did not, just that your tree was next."

"That's all that was told to Kennz? That doesn't make sense. How did she even see the vision?" Jax asked.

"I didn't say that it didn't show her anything else. I said it didn't show her what would happen in Mylo's tree. Plus, it was my tree that showed her when it handed over the scroll to Glipin."

"Okay….what else did it show her?" he asked.

"I know the order of the next three trees we will enter," I told him.

"The next three? If you know the next three then, obviously, you know the next four," said Margot.

Chapter 6 Kennz's Vision

I looked at her and shook my head no. "It only showed the next three, not the fourth."

"Who's did it not show? That then will be the fourth," Allie said.

I looked right at her and she knew right then that it was her tree that was not shown. "Why mine?" she asked. "What is so secretive with mine?"

"Nia, can you tell us the next three?" Margot asked, reaching her hand out and grabbing Allie's since she was standing near her.

"Mylo's, mine, then Jax's. I tried to find Allie's tree but I couldn't."

"Are you saying her tree doesn't exist anymore? It was there when we just left," replied Margot.

"I know, but in the vision it wasn't."

Allie then looked at me and asked, "What do you think that means?"

"Not sure, Allie."

"When we get to the trees can you use your horn or staff to see what is going on with my tree? Maybe it can provide answers to you then," Allie said, sounding more nervous and a bit afraid.

I took hold of Allie's hand and looked her straight in the eyes. "Nothing is going to happen to you or your father. I promise. I won't let that happen." I then turned to the others, "If anyone needs to use the bathroom or needs to grab anything, then do it so we can get back to the trees."

Chapter 7 Now We Know Where It Is

Everyone did what they needed to do before we left to go back to the trees. I could tell everyone's moods had become a little more serious, except for Allie's. She still seemed preoccupied thinking about what might happen.

"I need you to stay focused, Allie. I didn't want to say anything back in the RV about your tree, but I also don't want to keep things from anyone."

"I know. I am glad you told me, told us. I just wish I knew why and what it means. I promise, I will be fine. You don't need to worry about me."

On our way to the trees we saw what appeared to be a light show coming from them.

"What's going on at the trees? Could someone else be there and looking for the scrolls?" Margot asked.

"No idea, but let's pick the pace up and see what's going on," I said, changing into my Unistang form and then blazing a path straight for the trees. The others turned as well and joined me at the trees. The light show was still happening, but we didn't see anyone or anything else around.

"I think it's just us here. The lights seem to mostly be coming from my tree," I said transforming back to myself.

The others followed suit and we watched what was happening. Not really sure how to describe it, but it almost looks like the other trees are communicating with my tree using the colors of

Chapter 7 Now We Know Where It Is

their light to speak to each other. It was actually pretty amazing to take in.

"What are they doing, Nia?" Allie asked.

"I think they are communicating," I told her.

"What do you think they are saying?"

"I don't know, but let's see if we can find out." I summoned my horn and held it out in front of me.

My horn started glowing and seemed to be participating with the other trees. It did this for a few moments before it left my hand and started rising in front of me.

"Um, what's it doing, Nia?" Margot asked.

"I have no idea. I'm no longer controlling it. It won't even allow me to feel what is happening either."

"Were you able to feel or see anything before it started floating?" she asked me.

"No. It's like it didn't want me to understand anything it was doing."

Jax walked over to me and asked, "Can you summon your staff and see if you can control them as the Grand Mermaid?"

It was an interesting thought. Maybe he was on to something. "I will become the Grand Mermaid and be older for the time being," I told him.

"I know, but if it's going to help us out then I think it's worth it," he said.

"Well then, I think it's worth a shot." I looked at my right forearm and held out my arm in front of me summoning my staff. I did change, but not as the Grand Mermaid...I simply became an older version of myself. Once I did this my horn disappeared altogether.

Chapter 7 Now We Know Where It Is

I wasn't sure what to do so I held my staff out high in front of me. It began to glow and shake in my hand. I wasn't about to let it go since I didn't want the same thing that happened to my horn to happen to my staff.

The staff was really moving in my hand and started to spin. I quickly grabbed hold of it with my other hand, too. It was spinning faster and faster and was becoming more difficult to control. Jax saw that I was losing my grip on it and ran over to help me hold it. He put his hands on the staff to help me control it and it immediately stopped spinning. I looked at him and he at me.

"Well that was easier than I thought it would be," he told me.

Just then the staff shot a light at Allie's tree knocking Jax and myself backwards onto the ground. My staff was floating above the ground and focused its light onto her tree. The six of us stared at it and then something happened...Allie's tree was gone.

"What happened to my tree?" Allie frantically shouted out.

Before anyone could answer, my staff turned and faced Jax's tree and shot a light towards it. We then saw a miniature version of Allie's tree come out of my staff and was immediately absorbed into his tree. My staff stopped glowing and fell to the ground.

The others looked at Jax and me while we were staring at my staff on the ground and then each other. "What was that all about, Nia?" Allie asked a bit angered sounding like this was my fault.

I said the only thing that came to me, "At least we know why I couldn't see your tree in the vision that Kennz had."

Chapter 7 Now We Know Where It Is

Just then Mylo's tree began to glow diverting our attention now onto it. The lock on his door fell off and the door opened up without any of us having to do anything to make that happen. Jax and I quickly stood up and walked over to where my staff was and picked it up. I absorbed it into my forearm just so Allie wouldn't think I was responsible for anything else that might happen...even though I really didn't have any control over the last thing that happened.

The others walked over to us.

"Any ideas of what just happened, Nia?" a still angry Allie asked.

"Allie, I'm going to be honest with you...I had no control over what was happening."

"You couldn't stop it?" she asked.

"Did you not see Jax and I doing everything we could just to try and hold onto the staff? I have no idea why it did that. I'm sure, though, it had a perfectly good reason for it."

"Yeah! Like what?"

I looked at her and really had no answer for her.

"I thought so," she said to me.

"Hey, Allie. Why are you so angry with Nia? It's not like she is controlling any of this." Jax said to her.

"No, but she did make all of this happen."

"That's not fair!" I exclaimed to her. "Don't you think that if I could remember why I did any of this that we would be going through this charade? I'm just as confused as you are. Right now, though, I think we should get inside Mylo's tree before it locks us out."

Allie began to cry and then came up to me and threw her arms around me giving me a hug.

Chapter 7 Now We Know Where It Is

"I'm so sorry, Nia. I don't know what came over me."

"I know how anxious you are about all this," I said to her, consoling her. "We are all a bit on edge, but we're in this together and we've got each others backs."

The others gathered around her and we had a group hug moment. It didn't last very long, though, as a strong tornado like wind swirled out of Mylo's tree and quickly rounded us up and pulled us in. After being pulled past the threshold the door slammed, but this time we were all back in a very familiar place. A few of us bonked our heads on a few of the cabinets.

"That smarted," remarked Allie.

We helped each other up and quickly perused our surroundings before doing anything else.

Chapter 8 Proving Her Wrong

It seems like we all had the same thought. We ran over to the drawers to see if there was anything new in our folders. When we opened the drawers, to our surprise, there were no folders in there. In fact, there was nothing in the drawers.

"Looking for something, morpions?" a strong female voice asked us.

"Mom, is that you???" Mylo yelled out, confused by what he was looking at. "What or who are you?"

"First off, young man, I am not your mom, you filthy looking morpion. All of you. I would never associate with one of you. Show your true

Chapter 8 Proving Her Wrong

colors," she told him and then changed into her form taking the identity of a tigaroo letting out a ferocious roar. Her fangs were sharp, able to devour whatever she caught. Her looks were intimidating as she stood standing in front of us on her hind legs balancing on her powerful tail.

"Here we go again with the parental identity issues," Margot quipped.

"Who said that?" she asked, pointing one paw at us releasing the claws from within.

No one said anything so I spoke. "Who are you?" I asked, in my most congenial voice.

"I am Leilani, the ruler of all land animals, and the keeper and protector of the Archive Room. And you are all," she was saying when Margot interrupted her.

"Trespassing...Yeah, we know."

Leilani looked at her a bit shocked. "Young lady, you need to mind your manners. Interrupting someone with my stature is very much frowned upon. I should have you exiled. What I was about to say, when you so rudely interrupted me, was that you are all not welcome here. We don't deal with morpions!" she exclaimed.

"Why does everyone think we're morpions?" Margot asked her.

"That's what you are, aren't you?"

"Ma'am, or ruler, not sure how to address you," I started. "What exactly makes you think we are morpions? Do we look like them?" I asked.

"Well, dear, you can address me as Ma'am. I reserve Leilani for my friends. And a morpion is a mole. That's all they are. They make good with whomever they are trying to destroy. When the time is right, they will stab you in the back."

Chapter 8 Proving Her Wrong

She then turned and looked at the rest of the group. "That's why I'm here, to make sure that you morpions don't get your hands on anything you shouldn't...not that you will be able to see anything on them anyway."

I looked at the others and they pretty much shrugged their shoulders at me. I thought for a moment or two and then said to her, "What if we could?"

"If you could what, deary?" Leilani asked.

"What if we could see what was on those folders? Or maybe you're protecting a scroll. What if we could tell you what was on there?"

She looked me up and down very curiously and then approached me, "You are older than them and they seem to look to you for some sort of guidance. You don't look all that special to me. Tell me your name!" she demanded.

"When did you become so cynical?" asked Mylo.

She really didn't seem too concerned about what Mylo had just asked and, instead, kept her focus on me.

"Your name?" she demanded again.

I turned looking at the others. Most of them shrugged their shoulders, again, except for Jax. He smiled and nodded his head yes. I then turned back towards Leilani and proclaimed, "My name is Shiloh and those scrolls belong to me."

Leilani didn't look all that surprised. She then circled me a few times before stopping and saying, "You are not Shiloh. I know Shiloh and she would have recognized me. You may look like her, but you are not her."

She circled me a few more times and then spoke again, "Your name is Nia. You are the one

Chapter 8 Proving Her Wrong

foretold about who will come and seek out the scrolls."

"How do you know this?" I asked, a bit shocked.

She put her hand out in front of her. One of my journals appeared in her hand. "It is written in these pages," she said handing it to me.

I had a very curious and alarming look on my face when she presented it to me. "How did you get in possession of this?"

"It was found right outside these walls. The morpion was trying to gain access to the room when he became frustrated. I'm assuming he threw it to the ground in disgust when he realized he could not get in here," she explained.

"Why would he have just left it here?" I asked.

She then grabbed it from me and opened it up turning to a particular page. "It could be because of what is on this page," she said, while pointing at a picture.

"What is it, Nia?" Allie asked.

"It's a drawing of the old school symbol and then a few other symbols that I don't know what they mean. There's also the name of the this room A18 – the Archive Room," I replied.

The others came over to look at it.

"Did you draw that, Nia?" asked Jax.

"I must have." I then perused the other pages of the journal a few times trying to remember anything I could from it. "I don't remember writing any of this," I said aloud.

I kept looking through it until I stopped when I saw something that was written on one of the pages. It reads as follows:

Chapter 8 Proving Her Wrong

'My true form will be revealed again to me by the time I reach 18 and return to Forest Creek. I will seek out the pieces of the SWOOZL and make them one. I will then use the SWOOZL to unite the Golden Scroll with the Onyx Diamond and release its power to restore the land I call Forest Creek.'

I closed the journal and looked at Leilani. "So this is how he knew. This is the reason for the bounty. He knew that I would be coming back, but then, so did I...but, how?"

I broke from the others and walked about the room with the journal in my hand. I looked at it a few times shaking my head while trying to remember.

"Nia, are you alright?" Margot asked.

I stopped and turned to the group. "You already know... I wish I could remember all of this. I'm holding something in my hand that belongs to me, but have no idea about anything that I wrote in it or even when I wrote it."

A page then dropped from my journal floating slowly, swaying back and forth, before it hit the ground. I knelt down to pick it up when I noticed another drawing I had made. I stayed kneeling looking at the picture. I then turned to Leilani and then the others.

"What is it, Nia?" Mylo asked, walking over to me extending his hand to help me stand back up.

"Thank you, Mylo." I turned the picture for the others to see.

"Is that the lake?" Allie asked.

"It looks like it," I told her.

Jax pointed to something on the page and asked, "What are those two things you drew by you?"

Chapter 8 Proving Her Wrong

I brought the page closer to get a better look. I studied it over for a moment and then put it down. I put my hand to my forehead.

"What is it?" Jax asked.

I took my hand away and looked at Jax. "That's not me."

"Then who is it?" he asked.

"I think that is the boy and those items...one is a piece of the SWOOZL and the other is a scroll.

"You showed him a scroll, too?" Jax asked in disbelief.

"Yeah! I'm assuming I did. I must have," I said, a little taken back.

"Then that's what my dad meant when he told us that the last scroll could also be obtained from someone other than us," Margot said.

"Wait a minute," Kennz started to say. "Does that mean he has a scroll?"

I looked at her and shook my head saying, "I don't know, Kennz. I really don't know."

"Hand me the journal please, Nia," Jax told me.

I handed it over to him and asked, "What do you want it for?"

"To see if there is anything else in here that might be able to give us more information."

Before Jax was able to get very far into the journal, Leilani turned back into her human form and quickly snatched the journal out of Jax's hands.

"You may not be morpions after all," she said, looking at us. "Before I let you see anymore of what is in this journal, you must prove yourself."

I took a deep breath and looked her straight in her eyes asking, "What is it that you want us to do?"

Chapter 8 Proving Her Wrong

"If you are who you really say you are then I will let you have that which you seek, but you must first tell me what this means."

She turned to one of the pages where there was a symbol with three words written above it. The symbol was familiar but the words were in a different language. They were written in Latin.

I looked at the page and then back at Leilani. "The symbol is a trick," I told her.

"The symbol is not a trick. I guess you are not worthy of what it is that you seek," she replied.

Before she could pull back the journal I put my hand over it and the symbol changed to the new symbol of the school.

"Impressive, my dear. It looks like you have a bit of wizardry in you as well." She noticed the words did not change. "Unfortunately, if you cannot tell me what the words mean, then you don't get what you came for."

I studied the words but nothing was coming to me. I could then feel the hovering of the others over my shoulders trying to get a peek.

"What are the words? I can barely see them," asked Allie.

"It reads 'Custodire – Docere – Evolve'. The last word is pretty easy to figure out."

I could hear the others whispering to each other trying to figure out what the other two words said.

"Time is about up, deary. Do you know what it says? You should know if you really are the one that put it there," Leilani remarked.

I put my hand over it one more time, but this time I felt another hand on top of mine. I

Chapter 8 Proving Her Wrong

looked to see whose it was and noticed that it was Mylo's.

"I figured you could use another hand," he said, smiling at me.

I smiled back. "I certainly can. Do me a favor and close your eyes and concentrate on the words," I told him.

Mylo then closed his eyes while I did the same. I could feel the charge of Mylo's energy as he focused in on the words. Our hands hovered over the words for only a few seconds when it occurred to me what I had written.

"PROTECT, TEACH, EVOLVE. Those are the words. No! That is the motto for the university, the new university," I proclaimed to her while Mylo took his hand off of mine while opening his eyes back up.

"The new university? What are you talking about?" Leilani asked. "I don't believe anything will be happening to this one!"

"That will be the new motto for the university, Mythical University. It will become the motto of what will reunite all the creatures of this land with the humans. And, no, there will not be a new university in this place. I just think that Forest Hills University needs a new name...one that will represent what we are all about," I valiantly told her.

Leilani did not like that answer.

"Never!" she exclaimed turning back into her tigaroo form. She then swung her paw with her outstretched claws at me. Mylo stepped in and transformed into his Taurix form quickly blocking her punch.

Chapter 8 Proving Her Wrong

"I wouldn't do that. It's not a good thing to be taking a swipe at your leader. I know the type of power that she has and trust me, you are no match!" he bellowed out to her, while holding her paw with his.

She tried to forcefully pull her arm back but Taurix would not allow it.

"I think she has proven herself to you. It is now time to hand over what we came here to get, unless you'd like to see me get really upset."

Leilani transformed back into her human form while Mylo did the same.

"You are mighty and brave, son. I am proud of you. You stood up and protected your leader – even against me. Your loyalty to her and this land will always be an asset you carry with you," she told him.

Mylo let go of her arm. Leilani then took a few steps backwards and pointed to one of the cabinets. I walked over to it and opened it up. Once the door opened there was a glow coming from within.

Before I could reach for it I overheard Margot remark, "No, Kennz, that is not another glow buggy thing either."

I let out a little laugh and then reached in and pulled the scroll out. I turned and immediately saw Mylo. "Thank you for standing up and protecting me. I do appreciate it."

"I will do it each and every time to protect you. You have mine and Kennz's loyalty along with the others in this room."

I took the scroll and handed it to Mylo. "You know what to do with this," I told him.

Chapter 8 Proving Her Wrong

Mylo transformed slightly into his Taurix form. He took the scroll and put it in his mouth absorbing it that way. He then turned back into Mylo. We looked at him very strangely.

"What?" he asked, looking at us.

I just shook my head at him. "Is there ever a time when you're not hungry? You know what...can you put this in a safe place as well?" I asked, handing him the journal.

Mylo again slightly changed into his Taurix form and gobbled up the journal. "I can't wait to see how you bring it back up," I told him.

"I just want to know where you store it," Jax said to him.

I turned to the others and said, "Let's get out of here. We have a few more trees to explore."

Leilani quickly stopped us before we left. "Before you go, there is something that I must tell you all."

Mylo looked at her and noticed that her tone had become one of great concern. "What is it? You sound worried," he asked.

"It's about the morpion," she began.

"What about him?" I asked.

"It's going to take a lot to beat him and obtain the last piece of the SWOOZL," she told us.

"Why is that?" Jax asked, pretty concerned.

"Nia, the drawing you made," she started.

"What about it? Did I give him the scroll? Is that what I drew?" I asked.

"We're not sure. The other Originals, along with Draya and Triddy, have all been trying to figure it out ever since we saw the drawing."

Chapter 8 Proving Her Wrong

"When did you see the drawing and how did you obtain that journal?"

"Draya gave it to us a while back."

"Of course she did," I said the more I thought about it. "I must have drawn that and told them about it on our way back home after one of the trips."

"You did. They were very concerned. Wesam called a meeting with the Originals to discuss it. You were still fairly young, so we knew we had some time to prepare. We put this particular journal and a few more in a few of the folders in the Archive Room. We do know the morpion accessed the room sometime after that – just not sure when.

After you guys visited the Archive Room and discovered that a few of the folders had been taken we knew that something would be happening soon and wanted to take every precaution to protect what was in here. You helped us out by changing the symbol to the room. When the morpion wasn't able to get back in here is when he became frustrated and threw the journal down and left. He mentioned something else before he left but I didn't quite hear what he had said."

"I have a question then real quick," Margot said, speaking up. "In the other trees we were in a different time up here. When are we now?"

"The time isn't as relevant as you might think, but if you really must know, the time is shortly after Nia changed the symbol. You see, the Originals have been following this journey the entire time. Once Nia was able to obtain the Grand Mermaid's abilities is when we lost ours," Leilani responded.

Chapter 8 Proving Her Wrong

"Don't you mean when I figured out that I was her and we became one?" I quizzically asked.

"Not quite, Nia. The Grand Mermaid still exists and you will have to figure out a way to fully bring you both together, again," she told me.

"What do you mean by again? We've already become one. I don't understand what you mean."

"When you all went through the first tree is when this plan was set into motion. The Originals were sent to a particular time and place to guard against the scrolls you are after. Once each scroll is obtained and you go back through the door we return without any of our abilities. Once you obtain all the scrolls the trees will fully become each of yours. It's how you wanted it," she explained.

"Do you know what happened to the morpion after he left here?" I asked.

"We tried to keep an eye on him the best we could. Oliver was able to get a beat on him and that is why we then spread out trying to find out more about what he was planning."

"What do you mean you have spread out? I'm not following," I told her.

Leilani looked at Margot. "That is why Oliver left. He was trying to divert the morpion's attention away from Forest Creek and see if he could lure him away so we could possibly catch him and locate Triddy. He created fake talismans thinking that is what he might be after."

"Did it work?" Margot asked.

"Only for a little bit. The morpion caught on to what Oliver was doing and then returned to

Chapter 8 Proving Her Wrong

Forest Creek, but not before confronting him and wanting to know where the real talismans were."

"That must've been when we showed up to your father's apartment around Christmas, Margot," I said.

"It was," Leilani replied.

Margot looked at her and asked, "What did he want with the talismans?"

"Those talismans are very powerful. Just as you can see certain things with them, Nia can see more when they are combined on your forehead. The morpion wanted them so he could obtain the power they possess."

"Is there anything else that the morpion is particularly interested in getting his hands on?" I asked.

"That is difficult to answer as I would only be speculating," she said.

"How so?" I asked.

"The Originals believe that there is a very real chance that he does have a scroll or at least knowledge of where it is or how to access it. If he obtains an artifact from each of you then he could use them to possibly get his dirty little hands on the onyx diamond."

"How would our artifacts benefit him?" asked Allie.

"Since the artifacts are derived from the different SWOOZL pieces, he could combine them along with the scroll and become very powerful. We just don't know how powerful he would actually become. If that happened he could summon each of your spirits, except for Nia's, back into Forest Creek," she explained.

"What do you mean by that?" I asked.

Chapter 8 Proving Her Wrong

"Each of you was born with a bit of the energy and essence of Forest Creek in your blood," she started to explain.

Allie quickly interrupted. "I thought I was the only one actually born here. Are you saying we all were?"

"No, just you, Allie. But the others do carry a bit of an essence and energy of this land inside their blood. It is what allows each of you to be able to use the artifacts that the SWOOZL has chosen for you; just like it was for the Originals. It's why Margot can be who she is but not her sister. It's why Nia is who she is but not Draya. It's all a part of being the first born of the next generation," she finished explaining.

"So, is Nia's mother more important than Nia...and I don't say that to sound mean, but was

Shiloh, or I guess Nia, the next in line to take her place?" Allie asked.

"Nothing like that. I'm not sure how to explain it, but this land, this area, the magic that lives here is and was always meant for Nia."

I wanted to find out more about this whole 'essence' thing so I asked her, "I know that my essence came from my mother because of her being from here, but what about you, Leilani? Where did your essence come from? Did one of your parents live here previously, too?"

I could tell that Leilani didn't quite know how to answer that question, but she tried anyway.

"I don't really know the answer to that. I don't believe that any of the Originals really know. We've never discussed why we were all here that same night that you, Draya, Legend, and Z were. We've assumed that, just like your mother, Nia, we

Chapter 8 Proving Her Wrong

must've had a relative who also once lived here, but nobody knows for sure. All we know is that we were the first born just as each of you were. I wish I knew more, but nothing was ever told to us by our parents. Even if one of them were different, maybe they weren't allowed to say anything just as we weren't. As for your essence coming from your mother...I believe it is the other way around.""

"How is that possible?" asked Kennz.

"Not quite sure, but Nia's mother knew it. When she discovered that this land was meant for Nia is when she knew that the presence of Nia existed before she did. It's just one of those things you have to accept and know to be true."

The others looked at me and all I could do is shrug my shoulders at them. I didn't really know how to respond to that except to say, "I think we should go now."

"One last thing before I go...Things will not be the same from here on out." And, with that, Leilani vanished right in front of us.

"What do you think she meant by that, Nia?" Allie asked.

"No idea," I told her.

"Now what?" Mylo asked.

"Like Nia said, we should leave and get to the next tree," Margot replied.

"There's just one problem," I said.

"What's that?" asked Allie.

"Not sure how we get out of here. That wind brought us in here. I don't think there will be any wind taking us out of here. It's not like we can open up a window," I told them.

Chapter 8 Proving Her Wrong

"No, but we can open up the door," Jax suggested.

I looked at him a little strangely.

"Didn't you hear Leilani?" he asked.

"We heard a lot of things, Jax. Where are you going with this, bro?" asked Mylo.

"Your mom told us that things will not be the same from here on out," he replied.

Mylo shrugged his shoulders and then asked, "Okay??? What of it?"

"I think what she was telling us is that how we entered is not going to be how we exit. This isn't going to be like the others. And, frankly, I don't think any of the other trees we enter into will be the same way we get out of them."

I pondered what Jax was saying and then agreed with him. "Okay. I don't see any other way out of here. Go ahead. Open the door," I told him.

Jax walked over to the door and slowly turned the handle. When he said that we go through the door he sounded pretty confident about his suggestion. Now that he has to open the door, he looks very cautious about doing it.

"What's wrong, Jax? Is the handle stuck?" Margot asked.

"No. I'm just.."

"You're just what?" she asked him. "Big tough guy Jax isn't so brave."

"Hold on will you Margot. Unless you can tell us what is on the other side of this door, I'm sure you would be careful in opening it, too," he told her.

"Oh come on, Jax. Would you like me to open it instead?" asked Allie.

"I've got it. Just give me a sec." Jax then closed his eyes and took a little breath before

Chapter 8 Proving Her Wrong

pulling the door wide open and then jumping back away from it.

I think we all expected to see the hallway outside the Archive Room but that is not where it led to.

"Is that the falls?" asked Margot.

"It certainly looks like it," Kennz said, being the first to walk through to the other side and then looking around.

I quickly followed, but before I went through I patted Jax on his back and told him, "You can breathe now."

I'm thinking that his heart rate came down about forty beats from where it was in just a few seconds. He finally let out a big breath. I know that we all are a little nervous and anxious going forward. This has been nerve racking for all of us.

Chapter 9: The Other Side of the Door

Jax was the last to come through the door which quickly shut behind him vanishing as if it was never there. We were back at the falls, but everything around us was of a grayish tone.

"Well, we now know which tree we are in," I told the others.

"Who's tree is that?" asked Margot.

"Mine," I said, looking at her.

"What makes you so confident it is yours?" she asked.

"Because of what's at the bottom of the falls," I told her.

"What's that?"

Chapter 9 The Other Side of the Door

"My horn!" I exclaimed.

"I thought the scrolls were found where the SWOOZL pieces were. What does this have to do with your horn?" Allie asked.

I turned to her and said, "Because I can't summon it."

"What about your staff?" asked Jax.

I put out my forearm and showed them how it can glow. "I still have it but I can't be the Grand Mermaid in order to get the scroll. I need to be Nia and the only way for me to do that is to get to my horn and transform into my Unistang form."

"So, how do we get it?" Margot asked.

"We jump in," I told her.

"No way...not again!" exclaimed Mylo. "You guys know I can't swim."

"Do we have to make that same climb, again?" asked a concerned Kennz.

I looked above the falls. "I don't think so, Kennz. I don't see the path."

"Wait a minute, Nia. That means we are here but at a different time. Maybe, even, before the falls and the lake disappeared," said Allie.

I walked towards the lake and stopped at its shore. I knelt down and put my hand in the water. Something didn't feel right. I then stood back up and looked all around me with a concerned look on my face.

"What is it, Nia?" Allie asked, walking up to me.

"This doesn't feel right. Something's off. I just don't know what it is." I began to walk over to where the others were, thinking that Allie was next to me. I turned back and saw her still standing near the shore not moving.

"Allie, what are you doing?" I asked.

Chapter 9 The Other Side of the Door

There was no response from her so I said it again thinking she didn't hear me.

"Allie, are you coming back over here?" I asked pretty loud.

No response from her.

"I don't like this," I told the others. We then ran towards her.

She turned around right before we got to her.

"Whew! We thought something had happened to you," I said. "What were you doing?"

In a strange voice she responded, "You are not welcome here. Leave now before it's too late."

"Allie?" Kennz yelled out.

"That's not Allie. That's the voice of the morpion," I said.

Allie then transformed, but not just as her Owl form...she had a little dragon mixed in. She had formed a long dragon's tail with spikes all over it.

"Last chance...LEAVE!" she exclaimed and then blew some fire at us before flying away but vanishing just as quick.

"Umm, that's not a good thing. She's now part dragon AND she can disappear at will," Jax replied

"Now I know...but I wonder what triggered it?" I said aloud.

"You know what?" Jax asked.

"A while back Wesam and Draya pulled me aside and indicated that there might be more to Allie...that she might have another artifact that she's not aware of."

"Why now? And, how did she transform when we are in your tree. No one else has been

Chapter 9 The Other Side of the Door

able to do that in any of the other trees," Mylo remarked.

"I thought that seemed strange, too, Mylo. I don't know why she was able to add the dragon part." I thought about it for a few more seconds and an idea came to me. "Everyone try changing and see what happens."

The others looked strangely at me, but then spread out. They immediately were able to change into their forms, but I wasn't. I even tried summoning my staff thinking that I could change into the Grand Mermaid, but I wasn't able to.

They quickly changed back into their human forms.

"Why is it that we can change, but you can't, considering this is your tree?" asked Jax.

"I think it has to do with what Leilani told us about things not being the same. I'm thinking this is one of them."

"What else do you think she meant?" asked Margot.

"No idea, but I'm sure we're going to find out. Let's just keep on our guard," I said.

"Where do you think Owl or whoever she is now went off to?" asked Kennz.

"I have my suspicions," I told her.

"Then what are we waiting for, let's go after her," responded Jax.

"Not, yet."

"Why? We need to go get her!" exclaimed Jax.

"I don't think we can," I told him.

Chapter 9 The Other Side of the Door

"Wait! You think you might know where she is but we can't go get her? Why not?" he asked.

"Because, I don't think she is in this time any longer."

"Then when and where is she?" Margot asked.

"I think she is in her tree right back here; in fact, I think Jax's tree is also right here."

"What makes you think my tree is also here?"

I looked at him and walked over and grabbed his hands. "Because, I believe that your tree and Allie's are related some how. There's something about this location, this lake, that somehow connects the two trees together. Right now I need to figure out how to change into my Nia form instead of looking like Shiloh."

"How are you going to do that?" he asked.

While still holding Jax's hands I turned and looked at Mylo.

"Oh heck no. Really???" he responded.

"You'll be fine, Mylo. I promise," I told him.

"But you know I can't swim. How many times do I need to remind you of that?" Mylo then walked around shaking his head almost looking like he wanted to throw a little temper tantrum. I looked at Kennz and she immediately ran over to him.

"Remember how you stood up to your mother back in the Archive Room?" she asked him.

"Yeah, but what does that have to do with me jumping in that lake and probably drowning?"

"Absolutely nothing. It has everything to do with trusting her. She said you will be fine...you

Chapter 9 The Other Side of the Door

need to believe that." Kennz then leaned in and gave him a kiss. "Plus, I won't let anything happen to you," she said, smiling at him.

The two embraced and then let go. "Fine! Let's do this!" Mylo exclaimed.

Mylo, Kennz, and Margot walked over to the shore. Jax tried to follow, but I held him back.

"What is it?" he asked me.

"I'm not sure what is going to happen or who we're going to come in contact with, but I need you to know something...I'm in love with you. I have been for quite some time."

It went quiet for a few seconds and I wasn't sure if I just ruined the moment. I went to walk away when he held me back this time.

"I don't know how to quite say this to you," he started, "but I'm not in love with you."

I put my head down and mumbled "That's fair. I understand." I then went to pull away when he continued to hold on to me. "I wasn't finished," he said.

"It's okay, Jax. I get it. I understand. I need to accept it and move on. I'm thinking this is what got me into trouble in the first place," I said looking at the ground.

"Be quiet for a second please," he continued. "I'm not in love with you...I've fallen in love with Nia."

I looked up at him and smiled. "I'd kiss you but I wouldn't want you to get in the habit of kissing an older woman, so I'll just give you a hug."

I threw my arms around him and held him tight. I had the feeling he was looking over me when he tried pushing me away.

Chapter 9 The Other Side of the Door

"I think the others are waiting for us," he told me.

I turned and saw the three of them shaking their heads and laughing a little. "Are you guys done or do you need a few more minutes?" Margot yelled out.

I looked back at Jax. "Please give me a kiss when I'm Nia again."

"You got it. Let's go make that happen," he told me.

We quickly walked near the shore and the five of us stared towards the falls. I looked over and saw Mylo shaking his head.

"There's no way," he kept repeating. "I'm going to drown."

Kennz grabbed his hand and squeezed it tightly, glaring at him.

I knelt once again and put one hand in the water to see if I could feel the energy coming off of my horn.

Jax knelt down by me. "What are you doing?"

"I'm seeing if my horn is speaking to me and if I can feel it."

"Are you getting anything from it?"

"I sense it, but that's about it." I then stood up and looked towards the falls and then at the peak.

"We're going to have to get above the falls. We need as much momentum as possible to get to the bottom of the lake to get to the horn," I told them.

"Why can't we just stay here and cheer you on while you go after your horn?" Mylo asked.

Chapter 9 The Other Side of the Door

"Mylo!" Kennz said, while giving him an elbow.

"What? I don't feel like drowning today. Is there something wrong with that?"

"No one's going to drown today," I told him.

"See!" he exclaimed back at Kennz. "I can wait here and root for her. Go Nia, Go! Get that horn. You can do it! Rah! Rah! Rah!"

The four of us looked at Mylo and just began laughing. "Mylo, you're such a dork," Kennz said playfully to him. "But that's why I love you."

I finally stopped laughing and then walked over to Mylo. "Sorry to break this to you, but we all have to take the leap...again."

"NO!" he exclaimed, somewhat poutty. He then looked towards the peak. "There's no trail to get up there. No trail! No leaping!"

I put my hand on his shoulder and said, "We're not walking over there."

"Then how do you think we're going to get there? Even if I change I cannot jump that far or that high."

I turned and looked at Jax and pointed his way. "Krakalope will get us there, although Glipin will be able to glide on over there."

Kennz let go of Mylo's hand and changed into Glipin. She then ran back about fifty feet to get a head start. She quickly ran towards the lake. Once she hit the shore she leaped high into the air catching some air and riding it all the way to the platform above the falls.

Chapter 9 The Other Side of the Door

Mylo shook his head. "There's no way…" he was saying when Jax quickly changed to Krakalope and swept him away gliding on the water effortlessly. When they approached the falls Krakalope leaped into the air and threw Mylo to the platform. Mylo stumbled and fell to the ground. He then stood up and dusted himself off gesturing back towards Krakalope who was already heading back to the shore by this time.

When he arrived back at the shore he looked at Margot and asked, "Are you ready for this?"

"You better get me to the platform without throwing me or I swear," she told him.

Krakalope swept her out into the lake towards the falls. When they reached the falls he road it all the way to the top and put Margot onto the platform as gently as could be.

"HEY!!! Why didn't you do that with me?" Mylo yelled out.

"It wouldn't have been as much fun if I had," Krakalope yelled back.

I waited until he got back to the shore.

"Are you ready?" he asked reaching out one of his tentacle arms.

"I am, but we're not going to the platform. I need you to take me to the bottom of the lake so I can get my horn."

"Is that where the scroll will be, too?"

"I don't think so, but we'll find out."

I then was swept up in a couple of his tentacles. "Hold on tight," he told me.

We rushed out towards the middle of the lake with the others watching from the platform. Krakalope picked up more and more speed the closer we got to the middle. When we approached

Chapter 9 The Other Side of the Door

it Krakalope leaped high into the air and covered me up with a few of his other tentacles before torpedoing down into the water.

"Where are they going?" Margot asked.

"Who cares as long as I don't have to jump in there. Go, Nia, Go! Get that horn. Rah! Rah! Rah!" Mylo cheered.

I'm not sure how fast we were going but I couldn't feel any water around me... it felt more like air flowing around my body. We approached the bottom of the middle of the lake when Krakalope stopped and released me from his grip. My horn was right there where I had envisioned it. I swam over to it and quickly grabbed it. Krakalope encased me again within his grasp. He immediately surfaced to the top of the lake and then leaped towards the platform. When he landed he opened up his tentacles and then turned back into Jax.

"You're Nia, again," Margot said.

"I've always been Nia, Margot." Just then Jax grabbed me and gave me a kiss.

"What was that for?" I asked him. "Not that I mind."

"You said when you turn into Nia to make sure I give you a kiss.

I looked at myself. I didn't realize that I had turned into my younger Nia form...even though I was eighteen now.

"You didn't feel yourself change?" asked Kennz.

"Apparently not," I said looking at myself. I then realized I was no longer holding onto my horn. I figured that I had absorbed it when I made the transition from older Nia to younger Nia.

Chapter 9 The Other Side of the Door

"Thanks for not letting me drown, but why are we up here? Is the scroll around here? Plus, I was cheering for you. Did you hear me?" Mylo asked.

I laughed and said, "I did not. Next time cheer louder," I said smiling at him.

"Why are we up here, Nia, and not down into the water getting the scroll?" asked Margot.

"I wanted to make sure that I could get to my horn. I figured that Krakalope could get me there quickly. The last time I struggled making it to the bottom. I didn't want to take that chance again."

"So, where is the scroll?" asked Jax.

I walked near the edge of the platform and looked down. The last piece of the SWOOZL was given to me, well, by me down in a hidden cave. I'm assuming that is where we will have to go."

"You mean we do have to jump in there after all?!" Mylo whined.

"I'm afraid so," I told him.

"Bro, I can take you down just like I did Nia if you'd like," Jax told him.

"Fine! Just don't give me a kiss," Mylo quipped.

"There's no time like the present. Should we take the leap...again?" I asked everyone.

Jax transformed into Krakalope and put his tentacles out towards Mylo also making smoochy lips.

"Not funny," Mylo said, walking towards Krakalope.

I looked at the others. "Let's do this!"

Chapter 10 Not What I Had Expected

We took the leap jumping out away from the falls. On the way down Krakalope changed back into Jax while still holding onto Mylo. Mylo started screaming hysterically. I noticed Jax shrugging his shoulders while falling not knowing why he changed.

We were approaching the water at a fairly quick pace when I yelled at Mylo to plug his nose. He quickly grabbed it right before impact and closed his eyes. I'm pretty sure we all did. I expected to feel the water at any moment, but I didn't. Instead, we slowed down considerably and there was no water below us. It was completely different. The color had returned and we seemed to be floating.

I had seen this before. It was one of the times in my dreams flying through Forest Creek. I knew exactly where we were heading.

"Is this what it looked like when you went to the cave last time?" I heard Margot yell out.

"No. We're not going to the cave," I yelled back.

"Then where are we going?" she asked.

I looked around and pointed down. "Over there."

We floated through the air for a bit seeing the same magical colors I had seen before. When we started to descend the others had caught on to where we were going seeing the bridge just up ahead that I had visited numerous times before.

Chapter 10 Not What I Had Expected

Plus, this is where we had saved Spritz's mother from the morpion and his two person clan.

Once we landed Margot asked, "Why here?"

"This is a magical place to me," I said looking around. I then quickly ran over to the bridge. I took a step and that same wisp of smoke as before encircled my foot. I took a second step and the same thing happened with that foot. I then ran back and forth stirring up a screen of smoke encompassing myself in it until I stopped and the smoke dissipated.

Margot quickly ran over to the bridge and ran across it stirring up a purple haze with her steps. The others joined in and soon there was a plethora of colors all over the bridge.

"This is so cool. Has this always done this?" asked Kennz.

"It has with me. I didn't know that it could with you guys walking on it, too," I told her. "Pretty cool, huh?"

"Very cool!" she exclaimed back. "We should call this the Rainbow Bridge."

I stopped and looked at her. "That's a great idea. Good thinking, Kennz. Welcome to the Rainbow Bridge everyone."

Just then Jax stopped running and put one hand out to stop us from running.

"What is it, Jax?" I said, still feeling playful.

"What are we doing?" he asked.

"We're having fun!" Kennz exclaimed.

"Exactly, but that's not why we're here. Plus, let's not forget, we still need to find Allie and get her," he responded. "Can we just get the scroll and move on?"

Chapter 10 Not What I Had Expected

I looked at him and playfully stuck my tongue out at him. "Fine, it should be right under here where the SWOOZL was."

I walked to the center with the wisps still emitting with each step. I couldn't help but to be giddy seeing and feeling the wisps. When I reached the center I knelt down and looked over the bridge into the water. I figured I would see my reflection, but didn't.

The water didn't look cloudy or dirty so I wasn't sure why I couldn't see myself. I put my hand in the water and swished it back and forth. I still didn't see anything: nothing in the water and nothing above me – no reflections of anything.

"This is so strange," I said aloud.

Jax walked over to where I was and knelt by me. "What is strange, Nia?"

"Look in the water," I told him.

Jax peeked over the edge of the bridge into the water. He stared for a few moments.

"Well?" I asked him.

"Well, what?" he asked back.

"Don't you see it?"

"I see myself. Am I supposed to see something different?"

I leaned back over and looked in the water. I did see Jax's reflection, but nothing else. "Strange!" I exclaimed kneeling back.

The others came over to see what was going on.

"Hey, guys, do me a favor. Can you three kneel down and look into the water.

The three knelt down while Jax stood up and gave them some room.

"What are we supposed to be looking at?" Margot asked.

Chapter 10 Not What I Had Expected

"Just tell me what you see," I said, leaning forward grabbing onto a rail so I could see.

"I see the three of us," Kennz said, looking at me and then changing her look to a confused one. "But, I didn't see you," she said, looking back into the water and seeing the others plus herself again.

"Exactly! Why is my reflection not being seen?" I asked out loud.

"Hey, Nia," Mylo began.

"What is it, Mylo?"

"Weren't you going to grab the scroll?" he asked.

"Oh yeah! I almost forgot. When I couldn't see myself I kind of got sidetracked."

I leaned over and, again, couldn't see my reflection. I shook my head and proceeded to put my hand under the bridge into the water. I leaned in as much as I could swishing the water back and forth but couldn't feel the scroll. "It's got to be here. This is the same place I found the piece of the SWOOZL." I kept at it for a few seconds but couldn't feel anything. While still leaning into the water and holding a rail, I yelled up to the others, "Can one of you help me see if you can feel anything?"

I kept searching but didn't hear an answer or hear any of them move closer to me, so I asked again even louder, "Can someone help me find the scroll, please?"

There was nothing but silence. "Guys? Anyone? Don't all jump at once to help me," I was saying when I pulled myself up and noticed that the others were no longer by me or on the bridge.

"Guys?" I said in a little softer voice standing up.

Chapter 10 Not What I Had Expected

I looked around and couldn't find them. "Okay, this isn't funny. You can all come out now," I said as I started walking across the bridge to the same side we started on. "Why are there no wisps when I walk on here any longer?" I then looked around and noticed that the color was disappearing around me and everything was turning all shades of gray just as it was when we entered into my tree. I watched as the last of the color had faded right in front of me. By this time I was starting to lose all hope. Why would I have done this? Why would I have made it so difficult to get something that was meant for me? I started to think for a few moments that maybe I did all of this because I really didn't want myself to find the scrolls.

"What's going on? Where is everyone?"

Everything around me started closing in on me. I immediately ran back onto the bridge and then over to the other side. I turned back and saw that the bridge had also disappeared. I was now standing on a makeshift island that was surrounded by the creek. I had to do something. I looked down at my arm but couldn't summon my staff. I tried for my horn, but ended up with the same result as the staff. I walked over near the creek, but wasn't allowed to get to close to it. It was almost like something was preventing me from getting near the water. I walked back towards the middle of the island and stopped. I turned around one last time completing a full turn. I felt abandoned and alone. I wasn't scared, but I was definitely having some reservations about what was happening. This tree was clearly not like the others we had been in. I knew that I needed to figure out how to get the golden scroll and then move onto the next one and find the others.

Chapter 10 Not What I Had Expected

"Believe, Nia. Believe," I heard someone telling me. "Believe, Nia. Believe," I heard again, but coming from a different voice.

"Believe! Believe! Believe!" many voices were now shouting at me.

I spun around in circles trying to figure out where all the voices were coming from. Louder and louder they tolled, eventually knocking me to the ground whilst covering my ears.

Then they stopped. Complete silence. I got to one knee. Everything was still a grayish dull tone. I was able to see the creek, but the water stayed still.

I pushed myself up and then walked as close to the creek as was allowed. I could feel where the force was pushing back on me. I looked into the water, but there was still no movement coming from it. I hung my head now cradling it with my hands. Maybe I'm not the person that everyone is making me out to be. The doubt was growing stronger the longer I was here. I grew tired and leaned up against the invisible force preventing me from moving forward. I stayed like this for about twenty minutes or so until I felt a weird energy, a presence of some sort that was behind me and then heard, "Nia, you need to believe!"

Chapter 11 It's Not Black Nor White

I turned around slowly knowing that this was no longer just a voice, but had a form to them. It was the Grand Mermaid, but she was now standing in my mirror that was now on the island.

"What is happening?" I asked, in a very weak and tired voice. "I don't know if I can do this."

The Grand Mermaid stepped out of the mirror, but she wasn't alone. The younger five year old version of me stepped out after her...then the fourteen year old version. Then, pretty much every version of me until the age that Shiloh was before setting all of this into motion.

"What is this?" I asked her.

The Grand Mermaid came over and walked by me kneeling down and getting some water from the creek. "Drink this," she told me.

I looked at her, confused, putting my hand out but still feeling the resistance of the invisible force on me. "How did you do that?"

"Just drink this," she said, handing me a cup with some of the creek water in it.

I put a finger in the cup to make sure the water was real. There was still no movement from the water, but nonetheless, it was water. I drank it quickly and started to regain a little energy.

"Can you tell me what is happening? Do I need to go through some test in order to get the scroll? Why are there all these iterations of me here? Why haven't you been giving me any help?

Chapter 11 It's Not Black Nor White

Why did I do all of this?" I asked, stepping away from her.

She looked at me for a moment without saying anything. I knew she was giving me some time to cool down and compose myself.

"Nia, this isn't about the scrolls. This isn't about the SWOOZLs," she started to tell me.

"Then what is it about? Ever since this began everyone keeps dancing around the questions I have and no one will really give me a straight answer to any of them. Why? I know what I did and want to fix it, but why did I make it so difficult on myself and my friends?"

"Do you know why all of us are here, Nia? Why we stepped out of that mirror?"

"I have no idea..why?"

"We are all you...but we are NOT you," she told me.

"That makes no sense," I said, walking around all of the other me's.

"Fine!" the Grand Mermaid exclaimed walking up to one of the other me's. She then had one of the younger versions of me take a step forward. "Tell me about this one."

I walked in front of her and stood there for a few seconds. Nothing was coming to me.

The Grand Mermaid then motioned for a few others to step forward. "How about them? What can you tell me about them?"

I looked at the others and then back towards the Grand Mermaid. "How is any of this helping me obtain the scrolls? I don't see the point. What difference does it matter if I can tell you specifics about them or not?" I need to get the scrolls, find my friends, and make everything right."

Chapter 11 It's Not Black Nor White

"How are you going to do that when you don't even know who you are, yet?" she poignantly asked. "See, Nia, what you are seeing is very representative of who you are right now."

"You're telling me that all of…, well, them is who I am right now?"

"No, Nia. Everything else you see is who you are."

I looked around. "Everything I see is gray," I told her.

"Exactly!" she exclaimed.

I shook my head and walked away from her and the other me's. "Why can't I have a straightforward answer from anyone?"

I waited for a response before looking back. Once again, I was the only one on the island. "This is stupid," I said aloud.

"But so true," I heard a voice exclaim to me coming out of thin air.

I threw my hands up in the air and sat down right where I was at not realizing I was close to the creek. I closed my eyes for a few moments just to try and collect my thoughts. When I opened them I was no longer on the island, but now at my favorite spot next to the creek near spot T-19. I saw the water and turned my body so I could reach my hands in it, but was stopped again by the invisible force that was preventing me from doing so.

I sat back down and put my hands to my forehead. "What did she mean by, 'so true'? Think, Nia. Think!"

I sat there pondering what happened on the island and all that the Grand Mermaid told me. What if what she was telling me was true? What if I really don't know who I am?

Chapter 11 It's Not Black Nor White

"You're getting it now," a voice said to me.

"What? How? I was thinking that. I didn't even say anything," I said aloud, looking around.

I waited for a response, but nothing. "Oh, now don't say anything," I said rolling my eyes. "This is so frustrating."

"Then figure it out. And, while you're at it, figure out why you're back at this spot," the voice commanded.

I looked up but didn't see anyone again. "Fine!" I exclaimed. "I will figure this out."

"Good! The sooner you do then the sooner we can move on from here," the voice answered.

I stretched my neck from side to side and then took a few deep breaths. "You can do this," I told myself. I closed my eyes and began to think about what happened and what was said to me on the island. I'm hoping this works.

Chapter 12 Confronting My Past

I took a few more deep breaths and really just wanted to clear my mind and see what came to me. In a few moments I was envisioning myself from the age of five through eighteen. I tried to see beyond that but I couldn't. It was as if something was stopping me; similar to the invisible force preventing me from getting to the water.

I started with my five year old self. I immediately thought about where I currently am – at my favorite spot here in Forest Creek. This was always my safe spot; the spot I would come to where I could get lost and interact with the creatures of the land...wait a minute, the creatures

Chapter 12 Confronting My Past

of the land. When I was five I would pretend that I was speaking with the creature of the land...no, wait a minute, I wasn't pretending – those were the actual inhabitants of Forest Creek I was speaking with. Those creatures are the same ones that Z told us about, some of whom we've already met. And those adventures we would go on...they were real, too. Everything I did up here, every time Draya and Wesam brought me here, it was to help me remember who I really am.

    At that moment a little bit of the color started to return overtaking small parts of the gray, but I didn't realize it, yet. Instead, I kept focusing on my trips up here and realizing what they actually meant. My mind then wandered to when I was fourteen and Draya, Wesam, and I took a hike up to the Overlook. My mind started to remember the story that we were enacting, the tale we were telling now realizing that it was their way of helping me remember who I was before. The Overlook, where I met my actual father, where the first piece of the SWOOZL was found, where so many places lead from and to. It also has that fantastic view of the falls and lake, that, at the time of our hike, I briefly saw but then it disappeared. I'm thinking there just might be more to those peaks and that view from the Overlook, I just need to remember.

Again, more color was coming back overtaking the gray that surrounded me, but with my eyes closed I didn't know that it was happening. I stayed focused on my memories and where they were taking me. I started to remember writing in my journals: what I had seen, whom I interacted with, and what I was able to do. The journals...I need to look at them again and see if

Chapter 12 Confronting My Past

there is anything in them that can help trigger more memories.

At that moment I began to feel a slight drizzle. I opened up my eyes and looked up. It was now nighttime with the moon directly above me. I didn't mind the rain coming down and hitting me as my attention was more fixed upon the moon.

My thoughts were now being taken in a different direction – almost as if the moon was making that happen. The rain started to pick up around this time. What was the correlation between the two? I felt like the moon was speaking to me, trying to protect me somehow, but what did that have to do with the rain? All I remember is that it seemed like during my previous camping trips up here, the hypnotic rhythmic pattern of the rain hitting the camper top would always help me go to sleep. Before doing so I would always see the moon through the dome like it was tucking me in for the night.

I opened up my eyes and shouted, "That's it...I'm starting to remember more, but I need to find my journals."

I looked around and noticed that the color was just about everywhere now. I then turned and looked at the creek and wondered if I could touch the water. I slowly put my hand in front of me and could still feel the force pushing back on me. I wasn't going to let it stop me this time.

"I know why this is happening and so do you, Grand Mermaid."

She then appeared on the other side of the creek directly across from me walking out of the mirror just like she did on the island. "Why is that, Nia?" she asked, already knowing the answer.

Chapter 12 Confronting My Past

"It was just like all the times up here before when Draya would put her hand on my shoulder or when I was about to land in the lake and Draya prevented me from doing so."

"What about those times?" the Grand Mermaid asked.

"I wasn't ready. I wasn't ready to touch the water, because once I did I would become you. Draya knew that I wasn't ready. Looking back now, I know I wasn't ready."

My other me's started to walk out of the mirror, lining up one-by-one next to the Grand Mermaid. In unison they all asked, "How about now? Are you ready?"

I looked at the other me's and then the Grand Mermaid, but didn't say anything right away. Instead, I kept pushing my hand through the force trying to stop me. I kept pushing until I was able to just about touch the water. I then lifted my eyebrows and looked intently at the Grand Mermaid. Before I made one last push to touch the water, I confidently looked at her and proclaimed, "I now know who I am. I am not you, I am not any of you, and I am no longer Shiloh. I am Nia – the rightful leader and defender of Forest Creek."

I put my hand into the water at the same time the Grand Mermaid and the other me's merged into one. They were absorbed back into my mirror which then cast its energy and light toward me before the mirror disappeared.

The energy flowed from the other side of the creek through the water and into me. A huge shower of blue sprayed out from me encompassing everything around me. White stars flew everywhere.

Chapter 12 Confronting My Past

The transformation wasn't complete, not just yet. I knew what I needed to do next. I threw myself into the creek absorbing the energy of the water that flowed through the land. I then stood up. My staff appeared in my right hand and my horn in my left. I combined them together with one slam. A great blue light emitted from the staff along with a tremendous boom echoing through the land. I leaned my head back looking up at the moon winking at it before melting my body into the creek and swiftly using its currents taking it back to the bridge.

I reached my destination in no time flat. Once there, I emerged from the creek back on top of the bridge appearing in my Grand Mermaid form and walked over to the center of it. I knelt down and reached for the scroll right below the bridge. I grabbed it and then stood up. The rest of the color slowly started to awaken around me displacing all of the gray. I saw the vegetation come back to life dancing while spreading out covering the land once again. The sky even turned from a musty gray into vibrant shades of blue and yellow. I think this was Forest Creek's way of speaking to me and acknowledging its approval. I knew the job wasn't done, but for a moment, this moment, everything felt right.

    I stayed there taking it all in and admiring the beauty that was before me. I knew this is where I belonged, where I was needed. I walked around touching the flowers, the bojo berry plants, and all the rest of the vegetation. I could feel the energy they were giving to me and me to them. Walking around, there was more bursts of color coming with every step I made; mostly blue but some white that was sprinkled in. It was just like my blue tree with

Chapter 12 Confronting My Past

the white encircling it. It is a reminder of who I once was, but also, who I am now and will be going forward. My two worlds and lives finally converged into one...the one I was always destined to be.

I knew I couldn't stay much longer and needed to bring the other four back so we could go find Allie. I walked back over to the bridge and took my staff and thumped it down smack dab in the middle of it. The others slowly started to reappear checking themselves upon fully reemerging.

"What happened to us?" Margot asked.

"I'm not sure," I told her. I then transformed back into Nia.

Jax looked strangely at me. "How did you do that? Why aren't you Shiloh?"

I walked over to him and gave him a little kiss on the side of his cheek. I then looked at the others. "I am no longer Shiloh. That part of me now lives in the past. I had to decide who I really wanted to be going forward." I grabbed a hold of Jax's hand. "We can do this. We can all do this, but we need some help."

"Are we going to go find Allie?" Kennz asked.

"No. We are going back to my house. We'll need someone who can help get her back."

I then summoned my staff and thumped it a few times. With a few flashes of blue sparking around us, we were quickly transported back to my house.

Chapter 13 The Journals

Triddy was the first to acknowledge that we had arrived back in the living room of the house. Her face turned to a worried one when she didn't see Allie.

"Where's my daughter?" Triddy asked, fluttering around and looking really worried.

"We're not sure, but we know that she is okay," I told her.

"And how do you know that?" she asked.

"Because your daughter is also part dragon and can vanish at will," said an upbeat Margot.

"She what?" Triddy nervously asked.

"She is part dragon," I began, looking at Margot slightly shaking my head at her. "That part is true. As for the vanishing part, I believe that she was somehow taken by the morpion. I believe that he is able to draw upon Wesam's wizarding abilities and was able to get her out of my tree and into hers. I'm still trying to figure out what ability I gave him."

Wesam, Draya, Legend, and Z all came into the living room overhearing what we were telling Triddy.

"You're right," Wesam was saying, walking into the room.

"Right about what?" I asked.

"You're right in saying that he is able to draw on my wizarding abilities. It all goes hand-in-hand with the SWOOZL piece he has."

"Are you saying that each SWOOZL piece has their own abilities?" Mylo asked.

"Not necessarily, Mylo. In fact, not at all," Wesam told him.

Chapter 13 The Journals

"Then how is he able to do some of the things that you can?" I asked.

"The SWOOZL pieces learn from what we do. Even though our abilities come from them, they, in turn, learn from how we use those abilities. Because I was the Wizlord, it stored my abilities. Now that he has the SWOOZL piece, he probably figured out a way to use some of them," explained Wesam.

"But not all of them?" I curiously asked.

"Probably not all of them," Wesam said with a wink and a smile. "I learned a little bit about them and figured out a few things. In fact, you were the one that showed me."

"Please don't say that. It's just something more that I need to remember, but I must know, what did you do?" I asked him.

"I put a time spell on the SWOOZL. It works by delaying when I have done things. In this case, he is just probably learning about certain things that I was able to do."

"Are you saying that he is now discovering all of your abilities?" Margot asked.

"No. In fact, he won't discover the majority of the things I was able to do, at least, not from the SWOOZL," said Wesam.

I looked at him a bit curiously. "What do you mean 'not from the SWOOZL'? Where else would he have learned how to do...never mind, don't answer that because I'm assuming the answer is me. Why didn't anyone just slap me silly until I came to my senses back then?"

"Trust me...some of us wanted to more than you know," Draya said chuckling and then gave me a snarky sister smile.

Chapter 13 The Journals

"I probably deserved that," I replied.

"So, what is this about Allie that we were overhearing?" asked Draya.

"She is part dragon," yelled Kennz.

"That's interesting. Remember when we told you that we thought there was something more to her that she probably didn't know, Nia," said Draya.

"I do, but how did you two know?" I asked.

Draya and Wesam looked at each other and Draya said, "We had our suspicions."

I looked at the two of them a bit skeptical knowing that there was probably more to it. "Come clean. How did you two know?"

Wesam looked at Draya and she nodded with approval back to him. "It was in one of your journals," he said.

"How did you get that journal? I wrote in it about a year ago when we were discovering our forms and abilities and...oh no...I hope you didn't see something else I wrote in there," I said.

Draya had a very confused look on her face. "I have no idea what you are talking about but I am strangely intrigued now to find out what it is that you wrote. I think you should share with us exactly what that was."

"I think we all are a bit curious – some more than others I'm sure," Kennz said walking by me giving me an elbow as she then looked at Jax – who had a very confused look on his face.

"But you said that you two read it in my journal. Wait a minute, I never wrote anything down about Allie also being part dragon. If I remember correctly, the only thing I put in there is

Chapter 13 The Journals

a question mark next to her form. I believe I put part owl and then a question mark."

"You probably did," Wesam began. "That's not the journal Draya is talking about, although I'm sure everyone here would like to know what else you wrote in it."

"Umm, well," I mumbled looking around the room. "That's not important. What's important is that we find the journal you are referencing. It's not the same one that Leilani had is it?" I asked trying to move on and deflect a little bit about the pages I wrote about Jax.

"It's not, Nia. Leilani kept hold of that one after we took it to the Council of Trust. Give me a second and let me go see if I can find the one we are talking about."

"You mean it's not back in the Archive Room?" Jax asked.

"Not this one," Draya yelled as she was already heading up the stairs.

While we were waiting for Draya to return, I was feeling the weight of the stares coming my direction from the others in the room. I kept ignoring them, patiently waiting for Draya hoping that she would be back down soon.

We waited...okay I waited. The others just waited for me to tell them. I turned towards the staircase and was wondering what was taking Draya so long. I couldn't take the constant staring so I walked over to the bottom of the staircase.

"Draya, hurry up, please," I yelled, rather impatiently.

"Hold on. I'm still looking for it," she replied.

"Don't you remember where you put it?"

Chapter 13 The Journals

"I thought I did, but it's not here," she told me.

Wesam heard us yelling back and forth and came over by me. "Draya, where are you looking?" he yelled up to her.

"In the closet where the unicorn stuffed animal was. I thought we put it right under the unicorn," she said walking out of the room to the top of the staircase.

"We did at first, but then I moved it," Wesam told her.

"And where would that be?" Draya asked.

Wesam looked at me and then up at Draya. "It's in the back of my underwear drawer. I thought that would be safer than the closet."

"You got that right!" I exclaimed. "Don't think anyone would want to look in there for anything."

"Why didn't you tell me before I ran up here to get it?" she asked.

"When you took off heading upstairs I figured that you had seen it in there and knew where it was. I didn't realize you hadn't. Sorry!" he exclaimed.

Draya went back in there and dug around to the back of the drawer where she pulled out the journal in question. "Found it!" she yelled out.

Wesam looked at me and rolled his eyes and then walked back into the living room where the others were.

Draya came down the steps and handed the journal to me. "I think you will find some things in here pretty interesting."

I opened it up and started going through it. "When did I write in this one? How old was I if you remember?"

Chapter 13 The Journals

"Oh, we remember. It was one of the few times we actually had to drive the entire seven hours to get home. You fell asleep on your bunk when we were about thirty minutes from the house. There was nowhere to really pull over and use magic so we just drove the rest of the way home. Plus, it gave Wesam and I time to discuss what was in there. You told us all about it the entire way. It was definitely one of the times you were really excited to tell us what you had written."

"How old was I?"

"I believe you were eight at the time. You were really excited to share with us what you wrote."

I looked at the pages of the journal and shook my head. "Huh," I sighed. "I don't remember any of this. Now that I think about it, I don't remember many of my other trips there with you guys."

"You weren't permitted to," she said.

"Why?"

"That's how you wanted it. Wesam would put a spell on you once you fell asleep so you wouldn't remember everything. You would usually get up in your bunk and we would talk for about an hour before you were out. There was a safe spot we would normally drive to. Wesam would perform the spell on you and then we would use the magic to get home."

"That doesn't make any sense. What was the purpose of the journals and me writing in them?" I asked.

"So the Council of Trust could see what information you were gathering and if it was triggering any memories."

Chapter 13 The Journals

"But if I was still allowed to keep the journals then why erase my memory after each trip?"

"You'd have to ask yourself that. I could only guess that...well, I really don't have any idea why you wanted it that way." Draya then put her hand on my shoulder. "Anything good in there?"

I turned a few pages and found the one that had an eight year old's version of an owl with a dragon's tail on it. "Here's the one about Allie."

"Anything else in there?" Draya asked.

Before we could continue, Legend yelled out from the living room. "Are you going to share with the group or is it just a party for two? Ladies, get in here."

I closed the journal while Draya and I walked into the living room. Legend had cleared a spot on the glass table for me to sit down by and put the journal on there.

"Is that picture in there of Allie as an owl and dragon?" Kennz asked.

"It is," I told her and then opened up the journal. I thumbed through it until I came across that page and then pointed to it.

"A real Van Gogh," Jax stated, laughing.

"Hey! I was eight. Cut me some slack," I jokingly responded.

"What's that next to Allie?" Margot quizzically asked.

"Probably an eraser mark that she didn't quite erase," said Jax.

"Probably," I said. I then looked at it a little more closely. I picked up the journal and held it closer to me.

"What is it?" Draya asked.

Chapter 13 The Journals

"It's not an eraser mark!" Margot exclaimed, looking at Jax and then sticking her tongue out at him.

I turned the journal a little to see if I could remember what I had drawn next to her.

"Do you remember anything?" Wesam asked.

"I don't," I answered still looking at the object. "I think it looks familiar. I just can't place it."

"Do me a favor and put the journal back on the table," Wesam said.

I pulled the journal away and placed it on the table like he asked me to.

"Okay, now close your eyes," he told me.

"You don't want me to hold something and raise it above me and then say something, do you?"

I playfully asked, with one eye open before closing it.

"I deserved that one," he said smiling. "No, instead, I want you to visualize the dragon on that page and see if it can take you back to the moment you drew it. Just close your eyes and focus on what that drawing looks like in your mind."

I closed my eyes and took a deep breath. I had a clear picture of the image I drew on the page.

"Try to remember where you were when you drew that," Wesam was telling me in a soft voice. "What were you doing? What was around you? Were you in the camper or sitting near the creek or possibly somewhere else within Forest Creek?"

I focused on the drawing in my mind and replayed Wesam's words over and over. I began to visualize me drawing on this page, but couldn't

Chapter 13 The Journals

quite make out where I was. I opened my eyes back up to get a better look at the object. I closed my eyes again and tried remembering. I could only remember drawing Allie as the owl and dragon, but couldn't remember drawing the object. "I know this looks familiar...I just can't place it," I said softly.

"Do you remember anything about the drawing?" Wesam asked.

"I remember drawing this, just not the object."

"Good. Do you remember where you were when you drew it?"

I opened up my eyes and picked up the journal again. "I don't. I just remember drawing it." I put the journal back down but close to the edge of the table. The weight of the journal on one side caused it to fall to the ground.

"No worries, I'll pick it up," said Wesam.

Wesam picked it up and placed it back on the table, but it was upside down. He noticed what he had done and went to turn it, but I stopped him.

"Wait a minute," I told him. I then grabbed the journal and looked at it while it was upside down. "This is one of the symbols I saw back in the Archive Room when I was looking at the folders trying to determine where to look for the scrolls."

"So it doesn't really mean anything right now since we already know where the scrolls are to be found," Margot said.

"It means something different, Margot. I saw this symbol next to the others. It has to be related somehow."

I grabbed the journal again and then looked at Mylo. "I hate to ask, but can you do whatever it

Chapter 13 The Journals

is that you need to do and regurgitate the journal or whatever you call it, please? I think there is something in there that I also saw that might help us."

"I've not had to do this before so bear with me." Mylo then stepped back from the others and this time turned full on Taurix. He put one paw to his belly area and then made some very interesting noises while gyrating his torso.

"I think I'm going to be sick!" Margot exclaimed.

Taurix kept at it until he was able to bring the journal back up. He quickly flung it over to us, but no one was brave enough to catch it. It was covered all in Taurix goo when it hit the ground.

Mylo quickly changed back and walked over to us looking very dignified in what he was able to do. We looked at him with all of us shaking our heads at him.

"What?" he said.

Margot pointed to the journal. "You need to clean up whatever that is on it. Gross!"

Mylo walked over to the journal and picked it up. He slurped up most of the goo and then used his shirt to wipe the rest off. "Here you go," he said handing it to me.

"Now I know I'm going to be sick!" Margot exclaimed.

I looked at Margot and rolled my eyes.

"What are you looking for in there, Nia?" Kennz asked.

"One sec...," I told her thumbing through the pages. "Here it is," I said pointing to an object on the page. I put the journal on the table for everyone to see.

Chapter 13 The Journals

"What are we supposed to be looking at?" Jax asked.

I pointed to a small drawn shape on the page. "That!" I exclaimed. "I believe that and the image in this other journal are connected. I just need a good pair of eyes to see if I'm correct." I then lazily turned towards Margot.

"Fine!" Margot said sighing. "Give me some space everyone."

The others backed away from the table as Margot summoned her talismans and her face shifted to Spidox at the same time I summoned my new staff. I put both journals side by side on the table. Spidox then hovered her head over the journals.

"Are you ready Spidox?" I asked.

She nodded yes and then I took control.

Spidox's talismans glowed a brighter color blue this time with a sheen of a blackish color around them. I focused in on the two symbols – one on each journal. Separate, I still couldn't figure out what they were. I went back and forth between the two and noticed there was a connecting point – almost like a puzzle. I looked up and, out loud, said, "I wonder...". I looked back down, once again, using Spidox's talismans to see if I could bring the two images together. They fit perfectly, but what did it mean.

I broke Spidox from my control and she changed back to Margot.

"Well, what did we see?" she asked facetiously.

I looked around at the others and then back towards Margot.

Chapter 13 The Journals

"Should I be concerned about the look on your face?" Margot asked me.

"No...at least I don't think so," I told her.

"Then what is it? What did you see?" she asked.

"The object next to Allie happened to be her glasses."

"Those were glasses you drew?" Jax asked.

I looked at him and put my head to the side and shook it. "I wasn't finished."

"Oh...sorry!" he exclaimed.

"Connected to the glasses was half of something, but I couldn't tell what it was at first. I then saw the image on the other journal that Leilani had. It turned out to be Margot's talismans with something connected to it. I put the two objects together from the journals and it revealed what looks like a map to something."

"I don't get it. What do my talismans and Allie's glasses have anything to do with the map or whatever it is that you saw?" she asked.

"I'm guessing that we will need to put the two together to reveal something, but what I wonder?" I turned to Triddy and asked, "Are you busy?"

Triddy fluttered right over in front of me. "Would this involve getting my daughter back?"

"It would," I said with a smile.

"Then count me in," she said.

"Good. Cause it's about time we head on back."

"Which tree are we going into next?" Jax asked.

"Yours!" I exclaimed. "And I have a feeling that the intensity is going to pick up."

"Why do you think that?" he asked.

Chapter 13 The Journals

"We're getting down to the last of the scrolls and it just dawned on me where I believe that map will lead us to when all is said and done."

"And where's that?" asked Margot.

"To the onyx diamond!" I exclaimed.

"If the morpion has Allie then we better get to her and her glasses before he finds out what they can do. I'm hoping that Jax's tree doesn't give us many issues and we can get the scroll fairly quickly," Margot stated.

"I couldn't agree with you more, Margot," I told her.

"Do you think it's wise to be going into Jax's tree rather than Allie's then?" asked Triddy.

"We don't really have a choice. The tree selection has been predetermined and there's nothing we can do about it. I wish it were that simple, but it's not. We have to take them in the order that the trees want us to," I explained. "Plus, Allie's tree is inside Jax's. Don't ask."

"Then we better get going. I want to make sure my daughter is safe and back with us – where she belongs."

"Spoken like a concerned and loving mother. Come on...let's go!" I exclaimed.

Chapter 14 The Council Code

Triddy was giddy with excitement knowing that she was returning to Forest Creek and would eventually be able to see Allie. While we were getting ready to leave to head back to the trees Wesam, Draya, Legend, and Z came up to us.

"There's something I need to tell you all before you head back," Wesam started. "And this goes against the Council Code that the Grand Mermaid established, knowing something like this would eventually take place."

"Are you sure you should be telling us then, Wesam?" Jax asked.

"Probably not, but I'm going to anyway. The last two trees may not be as they seem."

"We have already seen that with the other trees we've been through," Kennz interrupted.

"No...these are nothing like the other four. The last two are meant to deceive you all – so make sure that what you think you see is really what it is."

I looked at Wesam, "What is the Council Code and why are you telling us this if you're not supposed to?"

Wesam, in typical Wesam form, put his hand to his chin and then walked away from the rest of us for a few moments. I looked at Draya while he was walking. "Do you know anything about the Council Code?"

Chapter 14 The Council Code

"This is the first I am hearing of it. Wesam has never spoken about it before. I am curious as to what it is myself."

Wesam circled back around to us and then walked away shaking his head. He next walked over to the couch and sat down.

"If it is better that you don't tell us, then don't do it," I told him.

"It's not that simple since I've already started," he began.

"Are you obligated to continue?" asked Mylo. "I mean, it's not like the Grand Mermaid is going to do anything to you since Nia has fully merged with her...or am I wrong?"

Wesam was about to speak when we heard the rumbling of someone's stomach. It wasn't too surprising as to who we thought it was since we all looked at Mylo at the same time.

"What? That wasn't me this time," Mylo said.

"Sorry, but I'm hungry!" Jax exclaimed.

"There's a half a sandwich I made in the fridge if you'd…" Legend started to say when Jax took off heading straight for the kitchen.

This was probably the quickest...okay, probably not the quickest, but it was right up there, that we had seen Jax move.

"That boy must really be hungry to be moving that fast!" Legend quipped.

After hearing Jax open the refrigerator door we all turned back to Wesam to give him our attention.

"Whoa! What happened to Wesam?" Kennz asked, pointing at him.

Wesam was sitting on the couch looking a lot older. It's almost as if he looked like he was a

Chapter 14 The Council Code

hundred or so years old and somehow aged right before us...although he did it when we were watching Jax charge towards the kitchen and no one actually saw it happen.

"Wesam!" Draya yelled out. "What is happening?"

Wesam looked frail and was having a hard time getting any words out. He was even having a harder time sitting propped up on the couch. Draya immediately sat down by him and put her arm around him to hold him upright.

"Is this an action of you trying to tell us about the Council Code?" I asked.

We could see Wesam barely able to nod his head yes.

"Why did you make this a stipulation of speaking about that code, Nia?" asked Margot.

"I don't know. It's the first I'm hearing about it, too," I said, snapping at her.

"Can this be undone?" I asked, looking at Wesam.

He nodded yes, barely again.

"You need to fix this, Nia!" Draya demanded. "You did this to him."

Just then Legend and Z chimed in with Draya with all of them repeating and pointing at me, "You did this to him! You did this to him!"

I turned to the others and they began pointing at me, too, just as a green haze started to fill the room. Jax then wondered back in and changed himself into a young Wesam. "Are you going to fix me?" he asked.

"What is going on?" I asked aloud.

Just then the room began to spin around me with everyone still pointing at me, but now they

Chapter 14 The Council Code

were walking towards me. I began to back pedal but wasn't getting anywhere. Everyone else was gaining on me. I tried to put my hands out to stop them but they were being held back. The others were gaining on me and changing with every step. Kennz and Margot had briefly changed to Spritz and her mother but then changed right back. Jax and Mylo took turns turning into each others forms. I looked at Draya. She was still on the couch with Wesam, shaking her head, pointing her finger at me while yelling, "You did this!"

What had I done? Why would I do this? I had to make it all stop somehow.

Chapter 15 Jax's Tree: House of Deception

The green haze was growing stronger and I wasn't able to see everyone clearly any longer. It then dawned on me what was happening. I quickly closed my eyes and cleared my mind. I waited for the chanting and yelling to stop, which it finally did after a few moments. I then opened my eyes. We weren't back in my house any longer. We were in the forest where the trees are supposed to be. But, instead of the trees, each of us was standing where ours was supposed to be. The only difference was that Triddy was fluttering where Allie's tree had been.

Chapter 15 Jax's Tree: House of Deception

"Nia, what is going on? How did we get back to the forest and why can't I move?" Kennz asked, a bit apprehensively.

I looked around and saw the others standing there, somewhat frozen. I tried moving, but was unable to. Just like in my tree a weird force was not only acting on me but the others, too. I tried to move my mouth and noticed that I was able to speak.

"Is everyone alright?" I yelled out.

Jax was struggling to move and yelled back, "I'd be better if I could escape whatever has a hold on me, but, yeah, I'm alright."

Everyone else had similar responses. 'Something's not right,' I thought to myself, watching the others trying to break free. The more I watched them the more I became calm and started to feel the grip loosen. I kept calm and didn't move and within a few seconds I was free from whatever was holding me back.

"No one move!" I shouted. "Try to remain as calm and relaxed as you can. Once you can do that then whatever is holding you back will let go of you."

I saw a little fight from a few of them for a second or two before everyone decided to heed my advice and try to relax. One by one each of them slowly became free of the strange force.

"What just happened? We were in your house and then it was like something or someone took control of me and then I was a tree," Kennz blurted, pretty freaked out.

"Yeah! What was all of that back at your house, Nia?" asked Jax.

Chapter 15 Jax's Tree: House of Deception

"When you ran to the kitchen for that sandwich is when everything became weird," I told him.

Jax looked at me confused. "I didn't run to the kitchen for a sandwich. That was Mylo," he said pointing towards him.

I looked at Mylo and he nodded yes. "I'm sure you all heard my stomach growling. Sorry about that."

Margot looked at me with just as a confused look on her face that I had. "That wasn't you, Jax?" Margot asked.

"Why do you think it was me? Mylo just admitted to it."

"Because we saw you take off for the kitchen. When you were in there is when Wesam turned really old," Margot told him.

"I know! I was there. We turned around and noticed an older version of Wesam being held up by Draya. If I wasn't in there then how do I know any of that, huh?" asked Jax.

Jax and Margot started to get into it. "Knock it off you two. We need to figure out what's happening." I then looked around. "Has anyone seen Triddy?"

"She's right over...," Mylo was saying before noticing that she was no longer where Allie's tree is supposed to be. "She was right over there. I swear. I saw her there."

I felt a little finger tap the back of my shoulder. I slowly turned. "Here I am," Triddy proclaimed.

"Triddy, can you confirm if we are back in Forest Creek?" I asked her.

Chapter 15 Jax's Tree: House of Deception

"This is definitely Forest Creek, but different somehow. Just not sure how," she said.

I thought about those words, "Different...different," which I mumbled a few times aloud.

"What is it, Nia?" asked Margot.

"It's what Wesam was trying to tell us. It started back at the house."

"All I know is that was freaky whatever it was," Kennz said.

"But it wasn't real," I said.

"It looked and felt very real to me!" exclaimed Kennz.

"To me, too!" exclaimed Margot.

"I know it did, but whatever that was, it wasn't real. Just like Wesam told us, the last two trees will be trying to deceive us. Whatever we think we see may not necessarily be what that is," I explained.

"So everything around here could be a deception? Oh, this should be fun!" exclaimed Margot.

"Is there any way that some of those things may not be a deception?" Jax asked.

"Who knows at this point," I said. "I guess anything and everything is possible." I then thought for a few seconds, "Everyone...see if you can transform."

The others took a few steps back while Triddy flew next to me and was near my shoulder. "This should be interesting," she told me.

I looked at her and gave her a strange look, wondering why she would say that.

The others did their thing to transform, but were only partially able to.

Chapter 15 Jax's Tree: House of Deception

"Try again!" I called out.

Again they tried to transform, although this time was a bit different than the first. They did transform, but as one of the others. Jax turned into Glipin, Kennz turned into Spidox, Margot into Taurix, and Mylo into Krakalope.

"Told you this was going to be interesting," Triddy reminded me.

"Umm...what now?" Margot asked, after turning back from being Taurix.

The others turned back into their human forms awaiting a response from me. "Not sure," I muttered.

"Can't you do anything about all this craziness, Nia?" asked Jax. "You are the most powerful being here."

He was right, but I was incapable of doing anything at that moment. "I can't even summon my staff," I told him.

"You're telling us that since you have combined your present being with your past one that you can't do anything at all? I remember hearing something from Wesam or Draya that the Grand Mermaid was able to control all the artifacts and SWOOZL pieces at one time. Heck, we've all seen what you can do with Margot's talismans and how you were able to use Allie's glasses when she was captured. What is preventing you from helping us to control our own artifacts?"

Jax did raise a good point. Why am I not able to control my new staff? I felt like I was back at the beginning when I was trying to figure out how to summon my horn.

Chapter 15 Jax's Tree: House of Deception

"Give me a second to think about this," I told them as I started to walk around, thinking.

Just then Triddy flew over to me. "Dear, think about what Jax is asking you to do. It'll come to you." She then flew back near the others while I pondered what she just told me.

I thought for a few more minutes and then something came to me. "Let's go for a hike," I told everyone.

"A hike? How's that going to help?" Kennz asked.

"If I'm right about something, then you'll see."

"And if you're wrong?" asked Margot.

"I'm trying to not even think about that," I told her.

"Can you tell us where we are going at least?" asked Jax.

"To a familiar spot," I stated.

"Not again!" exclaimed Mylo.

"Not again what, Mylo?" Margot asked.

"She knows I can't swim," he said.

I overheard Mylo and had to let him know, "We're not going there, not quite yet."

"Then where?" he asked.

Just follow me.

We walked a bit until we came to the trail leading up to the Overlook.

"Why here?" asked Margot.

"I have a hunch about something, but need to see if I'm correct about it. Let's head on up."

We double-timed it up the trail. On the way Triddy wanted to see if she could locate any of the other guardian fairies that were guarding the Overlook and hiding within the vegetation. She

Chapter 15 Jax's Tree: House of Deception

began to flutter around sporadically saying that familiar "hum buzz" phrase the fairies make.

"Triddy, are you okay?" I yelled out to her.

"I can't find them...any of them. They're not here. I hope that morpion doesn't have them like he does my daughter. When I see him I'm going to give him the biggest..."

"Whoa! Calm down!" I told her. "You won't find any of the guardian fairies here, but I promise you that they are all fine."

"How can you say that? I haven't spotted a single one, nor have I seen any trace of them even being here."

"Because, Triddy, this place isn't really real...well, not all the way."

"Huh?"

"Just trust me. I promise everything will be fine."

We continued on until we finally made our way to the Overlook.

"Okay, we are here, Nia. Now what?" asked Margot.

I walked to the rail and looked out and started to nod yes. "Come over here everyone and tell me what you see."

The others joined me at the rail and gazed upon all of Forest Creek.

"It looks the same to me," Kennz declared.

"Look closer," I told her.

It was nearly dusk and was getting harder to see everything below us.

"Are we supposed to be looking for something in particular?" Jax asked.

"It's not what you can see, but more of what you can't see. What can you not see from here?" I asked them.

Chapter 15 Jax's Tree: House of Deception

Everyone looked closer until it finally dawned on Margot. "Where's all the water? Isn't the lake supposed to be over there?"

"Exactly. This happened to me the last time I came up here with Wesam and Draya, although it was a little different."

"How was it different?" Triddy asked, fluttering over to be closer to me.

"When I was up here it was about the same time of day. The sun was setting and the lights from all the campers and fires were illuminating the park. At one point I saw the lake and then it wasn't there."

"I'm not following. What does that have to do with any of this?" asked Margot.

"The lake has always been there, Margot, even when we couldn't see it. I bet anything, that if I head back down, the water will actually be there."

"And that will help us out how?" she asked.

"Not us...but, Jax," I said.

Jax overheard what I said and immediately asked. "What does the water being there or not being there help me out?"

"You'll see. Let's head down there and I'll show you."

"Couldn't we have just gone there in the first place and you could've just told us what we wouldn't have seen if we had gone to the Overlook?" asked a hungry and tired Mylo.

"I could have, but it wouldn't have proved a point about what is happening here. Just remember what Wesam told us about the last two trees deceiving us."

"Speaking of Wesam," Triddy began. "Can you help him to go back to his actual age?"

Chapter 15 Jax's Tree: House of Deception

"That wasn't really him. I mean it was, but it wasn't. It's all part of the deception thing that is going on."

"Is it possible, then, that what he was saying was also a deception?" Jax asked.

"I'm thinking that 99% of it was true."

"What's the 1% that you believe wasn't?" he asked.

"He said the last two trees would try to deceive us. I believe that this will be the only tree that will carry this out."

"What makes you believe that?" Margot asked.

"Because, I believe that the morpion is causing the deception here somehow, and when we are able to obtain the scroll, then that is how we will break it. The final tree will then become more straight forward."

"And how's that?" Jax asked.

"The first to the final scroll will be able to get the onyx diamond. The final symbol, which I believe will probably be the most important one on the scroll, will provide enough of a clue to find the general location of the diamond. I could be wrong, but I don't think so."

"Then why do we need the other scrolls?" asked Kennz.

"They will show the exact location and means of controlling the diamond. I believe that he knows the land well enough and will be able to decipher the symbol," I explained.

"I thought the onyx diamond could only be possessed by the one that is worthy to control it. Wouldn't the morpion need the other scrolls, too, if he wants to control it because he obviously isn't worthy?" Jax asked.

Chapter 15 Jax's Tree: House of Deception

"I think he knows of another way of controlling it, or he might use Allie as a bargaining chip if he doesn't get his way.

All along I have been trying to figure out what form I gave him. I always think that down deep I knew he wasn't just a human, but that there was more to him. Instead of giving him a form, I think I gave him an ability."

"Similar to what you gave Z?" questioned Margot.

"Sort of. With Z, she already had the knowledge of the land since she lived here. I think I just gave her a way to obtain more of it and retain it differently. With the morpion, I believe I gave him the ability to learn and to use what he has. I think that is how he figured out how to get Allie away from us and have her show her other form. I think there is another connection to her that he has, maybe through her father, and that is how he got her to show her other form."

"This all seems so complicated. Now I can see why you sent yourself back to try and redo all of this," Margot asserted.

That statement resonated with me for a few moments. The others started to walk back down the trail when they noticed that I hadn't moved from my spot.

"Nia, are you okay or is this one of those moments that you are stuck where you are and need help getting unstuck?" Margot yelled to me.

"I'm fine," I told her, then running to catch up with them.

"Then what were you doing up there because it looked like you were off in a daze?" she asked.

Chapter 15 Jax's Tree: House of Deception

"I was thinking about what you said to me about redoing all of this."

"What about it? You made a mistake and you now need to fix it. We get it and that is why we are here...to help you to fix it."

"But that's not why any of you are here," I started to say.

"That's exactly why we're here," stated Jax. "We are a team and that's what teams do...they stick together and help out their teammates."

I looked at Jax and could only smile at him. "But you guys are more than a team to me...you're my family. That's the last part of this that I couldn't figure out."

"That we are now your family??? That's kind of strange!" exclaimed Kennz.

"It goes beyond that, Kennz. You are the new replacements in a sense, but permanent. You are the ones that will be taking over the trees and the abilities from the SWOOZL pieces. You are the next in line and I had to make sure of it."

"Wait a minute...Are you saying this is all a test and that you will be doing this again in about forty or fifty years...you're going to be finding our replacements? I don't think I like that!" Margot responded.

"I don't really think that is the case, Margot," I assured her.

"And how can you be so sure of that? Sorry to say but you messed up once and took a mulligan on all of this. What if something else happens this time? Are you going to conjure up another do-over?" she asked.

"I can see why you are thinking that, Margot, but that's not the case. In the last tree I was able to choose whomever I wanted to be going

Chapter 15 Jax's Tree: House of Deception

forward. I chose Nia when I very easily could've chosen to be Shiloh again...although, I don't think that is what she nor my mother wanted. Margot and the rest of you, maybe I used the wrong terminology when I called you replacements. All I meant is that you are taking over for your parent..." I then stopped.

"We are taking over for our parent and then???" Margot asked.

"I finally figured the rest of this. The deception is actually the truth," I told them.

The others looked at me very befuddled. "How is deception the truth? We're not following you, Nia," declared Margot.

"I've finally figured out the purpose of this tree. I know it's a little confusing but hear me out. This tree is designed to deceive us...correct?"

Everyone nodded their head yes back to me.

"Okay. Wesam told us that we had to figure out what was really real and see beyond the deception. I believe what he was actually saying is that the deception is why we are here...doing all of this. I just realized that some of the deceptions aren't necessarily a bad thing."

"How is being deceived ever a good thing?" Jax asked.

"Follow me on this...You guys aren't the replacements...your parents were. This land was always intended for me and to share it with you guys. Your parents helped me get to a point, not that they ever deceived me in any manner, but what they were actually doing was somewhat of a deception that I had to learn from."

Just then we could hear the sounds of water babbling down the stream. We all heard the sound and rushed down the trail a ways before we could

Chapter 15 Jax's Tree: House of Deception

see the creek. "Keep going with your thought, Nia, because I think it is changing this tree and why we're here," Margot stated, starting to believe.

Before saying anything else I gathered my thoughts. I put a finger up to let them know to give me a second or two. I then began speaking again.

"When I found your parents and brought them back to this land, I knew they, too, had a connection with it. But, until now, I didn't fully understand what that connection was. It's each of you, the six of us. From Allie being the first to be born here to those so-called camping trips that we all thought we were on when you all met me here when I was always five years old. Those weren't camping trips, but instead to look like they were. Each of you are a descendant of Forest Creek and lived here at one point. That's why Draya and Wesam would visit your parent and why I was able to meet each of you. The deception was a good thing in this case."

More of the water was returning to Forest Creek and we could also hear some of the sounds of creatures throughout the park.

"I have a question then," Kennz started. "Why don't we ever remember living here? I know I don't."

"It's starting to all come back to me. After I devised this whole plan to start over and had Wesam turn me back to being a five year old, those trips that we took up here was to check on those that were still living here or who had lived here but escaped when I left. We would meet you and your mother or father up here to see if it was safe to come back to. You may not have been born here, but you always belonged here.

Chapter 15 Jax's Tree: House of Deception

My intention was to create a land for each of you to be able to live in peace. I promised each of your parents that I would do that. Things were going well until I gave away too many of the secrets to the morpion."

"Before you continue, Nia, since you are remembering everything can you put it all in chronological order for us? We've been getting bits and pieces, but since you remember, maybe you can clarify exactly what happened and when," expressed Margot.

"I will do my best," I said.

Chapter 16 Putting It All Together

I told the others to head down to the bottom of the trail and over near the creek next to spot T-19. I knew there were some rocks and tree stumps we could use as makeshift chairs. Plus, I wanted to make sure the water was real and that I could actually touch it this time. I wasn't sure if there was a force that would be holding us back from it or not. I knew that in order to get the next scroll one of us would have to get in the water.

Everyone found something to sit on. Before I began, I did go over and check to see if I could put my hand in the creek. Sure enough I was able to touch the water. I could now tell the others what

Chapter 16 Putting It All Together

I was remembering, plus I could feel that my abilities had come back.

"Before I begin I want to bring a few people here." I summoned my staff and held it up touching my forehead. I then put it to the side of me and struck the ground three times with it. Legend, Z, Wesam, and Draya had now joined us.

"What are we doing here?" Draya asked, a bit startled and confused.

"Yeah! Why are we here? Good thing I was dressed," Z stated.

"I apologize and know this might be an inconvenience, but I am remembering a lot of my past and want to make sure that I have it straight. Please, if I share anything that is incorrect, stop me and correct me. Will you do that?"

The four of them looked at one another and agreed that they would.

"Okay. Then let's begin...

The stories that have been told have pretty much been accurate, but I think the timelines have been a little confusing so let's see if we can put it all together and make sense out of it all.

Before I was born, my mother lived here as a mermaid with other mermaids, including Z. My mother is from here, but it wasn't known as Forest Creek back then. In fact, this area wasn't even known as the Whispering Pines Forest. I believe that designation happened a few years after I permanently started living here. The mermaids lived alongside the morpions. The mermaids were mostly water dwellers while the morpions stayed on the dry land.

My mother was the leader of the mermaids with Z as her general. Together with the morpions they protected the land.

Chapter 16 Putting It All Together

While swimming around one day in the lake near the falls my mother discovered an object but didn't quite know what it was. All she could feel was the energy coming from it figuring out that it had some sort of a connection to the land. She also discovered that it had another connection to something or someone, but didn't know to what or whom at first.

This object showed the mermaids how to harvest the land better, using resources provided by the water throughout the land, how to build, and it showed them later how to protect themselves against the morpions. The morpions were upset that my mother invited other creatures to live on the land and in or near the water; some of those being your parents' parents. The morpions were not in favor of this and eventually started a war with the mermaids. When the mermaids were able to stop the morpions most of them left, with the exception of the one family. They figured out how to blend in for a while without being caught. Unfortunately, this drove some of the other creatures of the land away while others stayed.

When the war was over and the mermaids felt safe, my mother and Z decided to leave the land for a bit to get away. After they left is when Z introduced her brother, Legend, to my mother. They fell in love and eventually married.

My mother came back periodically without my father. My mother tried to tell Legend about the land and what she was feeling but he didn't believe it at first. When I was born she brought me up here to test her theory about the other connection to the object. She discovered that I was indeed the second connection. She knew that she had to guard against the others from getting to the

Chapter 16 Putting It All Together

object, so she wanted to devise a way to have me find it when I was a little older but needed more items for me to find. Along with hiding the object, she hid five other items around the land that were personal to her – which turned out to be the first five artifacts.

Before she hid the object and the artifacts, she consulted the object for help. It created a Golden Scroll. She was able to use this one scroll to create six total scrolls from it which she wrote her clues on: one to find the object and the other five to find the five artifacts she hid.

During that first trip here with Legend, Z, and Draya when I was five, I found the first scroll and it led me to the object in the lake. This turned out to be the Mighty SWOOZL, but I didn't know at that time that it was part of something bigger. This was also the first time that the morpion boy saw me come out of the water, but as a human. It was also the first time that the Originals had come up here as kids themselves with their families.

The next time up here I found the first of the other artifacts. After finding it I galloped back to the lake and felt compelled to jump in it."

"Galloped? That's a strange way to say running, unless…" Margot began.

"Yes, I had transformed into a unicorn at the time…not a unistang, but a unicorn. After jumping into the lake is when I turned into the Grand Mermaid for the very first time. I swam throughout the campground, being able to change my size and shape depending on the water I was swimming. When I returned back to the lake I jumped out of it as the Grand Mermaid but landed in my human form. That's when I noticed the look on the morpion boy's face and knew I had to talk to him.

Chapter 16 Putting It All Together

I begged him not to tell anyone what he had seen. He agreed and on my later trips up here we became better friends connecting each time I came up here. Again, I had no idea who he really was at this time."

"I have a question, Nia," said Margot.

"What is it?"

"What were those five objects you found?"

I was hesitant to tell her or the others; especially with Legend around. "The objects were from my mother with one being a stuffed unicorn from her – the first artifact I found."

"So that's why you turned into the unicorn, but how did it know you could do that?" asked Jax.

"There was more to the object…a secret of sorts that connected my mother to it. I just didn't know it, yet. The other four artifacts were personal to my mother. She told me when it was time that I would know what to do with them."

"Can you tell us what they were?" Margot asked.

"They're really not all that important. They were little trinkets and items that she really liked that she felt a strong bond with and connected to," I explained.

"What happened after you found all the items?" Kennz inquired.

"That's when I moved up here permanently. Legend had seen what was happening to me and didn't know how to protect me at home, so he and my mother agreed that I would live here with her."

"That must've been tough on you, Legend," Margot said.

"It was at first, but I had Draya. We grew really close," he said putting his arm around her.

Chapter 16 Putting It All Together

I quickly ran over and gave Legend a hug and then Draya. I returned back to where I was and continued.

"I learned as much as I could about the land and area during my early years. I knew this place was special and I wanted to honor my mother by trying to bring in more creatures to the land. She was big on education and teaching. I knew one way to get more creatures to the area was to eventually start a university. After about a decade had passed, I knew I needed some help and that's when I was able to contact the Originals that were here that very first night when I was five.

I brought them in and we discussed how we could build up the land and protect it while creating a place for all the creatures to feel comfortable. This is when the Council of Trust was formed.

I was learning more about the magic I had and eventually was able to build a small university. The school became known as Forest Hills University. After I created the school, I spoke with Legend about him and Draya being part of this world. I wasn't sure if Legend would come because of my mother not being here any longer. He did, to my surprise, and it was nice to be able to reconnect with my sister.

My hope was to also bring in other regular humans and get the creatures comfortable enough so they would show their true identity without being fearful. I brought the humans in, but the creatures didn't want to show themselves, and instead kept their human forms around the humans.

We tried a different approach with the creatures. We enlisted their help so they would feel that they had more responsibility and a purpose

Chapter 16 Putting It All Together

to also being here. Because of them we heard rumors and rumblings of a mole in the area, but no one knew who it was. It was also during this time that I became closer with the morpion. I showed him how to use a SWOOZL piece which he eventually would obtain, I showed him a scroll, and I showed him where the Council met. He saw how Allie's father was made a Dragoninx and had asked if he could have a role as well. The Council put it to a vote and I was outvoted five to one. It was after this that he started to suggest that we move away. I didn't want to, but he kept putting more pressure on me."

"Did you guys ever leave?" Jax asked.

"No!" I exclaimed, shaking my head. "After finally letting him know that I was staying is when I found out who he really was."

"How did that happen?" Margot asked.

"I went over to his house and before I knocked I could hear something happening inside. At that moment they were in their morpion form. I immediately went back and gathered up the Council. We went back to their home and gave them an ultimatum: either abide by all the rules of the land or leave. They chose the latter."

"At least we know why he chose Allie's father to help him out considering he saw what the Council did to him," remarked Margot.

"Good point, Margot. I hadn't thought about that, but it makes sense now. I bet he was able to get close to him after that and started to control him with the SWOOZL piece he had." I then continued on with the story.

"After the morpions left, I thought we were in the clear. However, after a while, things started to happen. Allie's father was seen taking a few

Chapter 16 Putting It All Together

items and when we confronted him about them he denied everything. Plus, we were never able to find any of those items on him. We eventually stripped him of the title of Dragoninx and that's when we appointed Draya the next one. And then…"

I had to stop and take a deep breath while looking at Triddy. I could see her eyes starting to swell with tears and I did everything I could to make sure that I didn't start to cry.

"A short time later is when Triddy was taken. I knew who did it but waited for confirmation from Leilani and gathered the Originals to let them know what I had done and what I had promised the morpion.

Leilani and Oliver were tasked with tracking the morpion to see if it would lead them to finding Triddy. Orion and Zenith helped the creatures who wanted to leave Forest Creek to safely get out. Wesam and I came up with a plan to make me younger and go into hiding. I told the other Originals to leave and go into hiding as well. I wanted them to be safe while I was going to be growing up again.

    I also knew that I needed to do something with the other pieces of the SWOOZL and the Golden Scroll before being turned back into a five year old. I broke the scroll back up into the six pieces and came up with the plan that we have been living for the past few months. I let the Originals know what I had done but made them promise to never tell anyone anything – even me. Before leaving Wesam put a protective spell over the land, but over time, it began to fade. I'm assuming that is when the morpion was finally able to return without any issues. Up to that point, I'm thinking

Chapter 16 Putting It All Together

he was able to periodically give Allie's father abilities to move in and out of Forest Creek undetected. And now we are here...putting my plan into action in order to obtain all the pieces and restore this land."

It went silent for a few moments while everyone was taking everything in that I had just told them. Jax finally broke the silence and asked, "You said you promised the morpion something and that he was coming back for it. What was it?"

"It was the onyx diamond."

"What does it do?" he asked.

Legend cut in on my conversation. "The diamond enhances one's ability and, therefore, can enhance the Ternary SWOOZL to its fullest power."

"What did you call the SWOOZL?" asked Kennz.

"He called it the Ternary SWOOZL and he knows more than what he has been saying. In fact, all of you have been holding back."

"Those were your rules...not ours," said Draya.

"I know," I told her. I then looked at Wesam, Legend, and Z. "Thank you all for protecting the secrets. I know it wasn't easy and I put you all at risk, but I do very much appreciate it more than you will ever know."

"We know that. No worries," Legend said smiling at me.

Kennz sat there with a confused look on her face and then raised her hand. "I'm confused about this Ternary SWOOZL or whatever you call it and what Nia calls the Mighty SWOOZL. Is there a difference or are they one in the same?"

Chapter 16 Putting It All Together

"It's more of a technicality in terminology and understanding. Before the majority of memories returned, I assumed the Mighty SWOOZL was the most powerful artifact here. Now that those memories have returned I know the difference."

"So, what is the difference?" Margot asked.

"The Ternary SWOOZL is made up of three objects: the Mighty SWOOZL, the Golden Scroll, and the onyx diamond."

"But I thought you told us the object your mother found created the Golden Scroll?" she asked.

"It did. I know this is a bit confusing so let me see if I can clarify. The object my mother found in the lake turned out to actually be the Mighty SWOOZL, which I was simply calling a SWOOZL early on," I explained.

"So, it was the Mighty SWOOZL that created the Golden Scroll your mother used to create her clues," remarked Margot.

"Yes! When she consulted it, is when it created the Golden Scroll for her to use to write her clues on. I then used the Mighty SWOOZL to create the onyx diamond years later. The three objects together create the Ternary SWOOZL. I always felt there was more to the object and was finally able to figure out all three of its parts after the onyx diamond was created."

"I understand now!" Kennz excitedly exclaimed. "Thanks for clarifying."

Margot put her hand up but had her head looking down.

"What is it, Margot?" I asked.

With some hesitancy Margot slowly lowered her hand and then looked at me. "Not sure

Chapter 16 Putting It All Together

how to ask this, but what happened to your mother?"

I turned to Draya and I saw her wipe a tear away from her eye. I then turned to the others.

"I'm sure you have guessed that my mother is no longer living – at least in a physical form. Remember when I told you about those other four items she had me find?"

Everyone nodded that they remembered.

"Those items, those trinkets, were very important to her. She knew that she wouldn't be around much longer so she had the object, which turned out to be the Mighty SWOOZL, capture her essence and spirit into these objects. She said I would know what to do with them when she passed. When I summoned those artifacts after her passing, that is when they formed the onyx diamond. The first time I held it I knew she was still here. Her essence and spirit is that strong. This was her guiding light that she left for me, but I also knew of the power it possessed. Just like Legend told us, the onyx diamond enhances whatever it touches and makes it that much more powerful. If it gets into the wrong hands, it could become a very dangerous weapon. That is why I have separated the Ternary SWOOZL into its three parts, because when combined, it becomes the most powerful item in the land."

"How did the Mighty SWOOZL know to put the clues on the scrolls about the onyx diamond when the diamond hadn't even been created yet?" asked Margot.

"I'm assuming it knew that my mother was dying and what her wish was going to be. It created the idea of the onyx diamond and gave it its abilities before I actually created the diamond from

Chapter 16 Putting It All Together

her artifacts. After her passing I combined the artifacts with the Mighty SWOOZL and that is when the onyx diamond was created and became real."

"If I remember, I think that someone said that if the morpion got hold of the onyx diamond, and because he already has a piece of the Mighty SWOOZL, that he would actually have more power than Nia. Is that correct?" asked Jax.

"Somewhat," Wesam began, jumping into the conversation. "He would also need to obtain at least one of the scrolls. If that happens he would have at least one of each of the three pieces of the Ternary SWOOZL with one of those being the onyx diamond in its entirety. He would have enough power to pretty much do what he wants."

"That would be more power than having all the other scrolls and pieces of the SWOOZL? How?" Margot asked.

"It would be because he would have at least one of each of the three items instead of having more of the other two. It may not sound plausible, but, trust me, it is. That's why I separated all three of them," I told her.

Again it went quiet for a few moments. We sat there in silence reflecting on what was spoken about all of this. I then finally asked Wesam, "Did I leave anything out...any important detail or anything I might have missed?"

Wesam thought for a few seconds. "I don't believe so."

"By the way, I'm glad that you're not really old," I told him.

Chapter 16 Putting It All Together

He looked at me a little strangely, not understanding what actually transpired with him.

"I have a few more questions," Margot said.

"What are they?" I asked.

"They really don't pertain to anything except for you. What is your mother's name and why do you call your father Legend instead of father, if you don't mind me asking?"

"I don't mind at all." I then looked at Legend. "Do you want to take the question about your name and I will answer the other?"

"I can do that," he said. "I have Nia call me Legend because that is the name she gave me when I was able to transform my one and only time."

"When was that?" she asked.

"When Nia's mother passed away. We held a ceremony for her."

"What did you transform into?" asked Jax.

"I was part dragon and part merman. When Nia's mother passed she quickly became ash. I took the ashes up from the water and into the sky and held them out to the sun and then dove straight down back into the lake where I released them."

"Why take them up to the sun? I understand why you released them in the water considering she was a mermaid, but what does the sun have to do with it?" asked Margot.

Legend looked at me and I took it from there. "Because of her name. Her name was Eleanor – which means sun ray or shining light." I paused for a few moments and looked up towards the sky even though it was night now and saw the moon shining bright. "I finally get it. She is always around whenever I need her – whether day or night. She is the ray of the sun during the day and the shining light at night reflecting off of the

Chapter 16 Putting It All Together

moon." I then looked up to the sky again and whispered, "Thanks, mother." I gave her a wink and a smile. At that moment a cloud quickly covered the moon, but passed just as fast – as if it were winking back at me.

"So, what do we do now?" Jax asked.

"I'm glad you asked me that. Do me a favor and grab me and jump into the creek."

Jax didn't realize that he would be able to transform into his Krakalope form. "I'm sorry...you want me to do what?"

"You heard me just fine."

"But…" he started.

"Trust me!" I exclaimed.

"Are you guys going to have to defeat his father somehow in order to obtain the scroll?" Margot asked.

"Nope!" I announced very confidently.

"Why is that? We've met an Original in every tree and had to go through them to get the scroll somehow," Margot remarked.

"We'll be fine. We'll meet him, but there won't be an issue. I can just feel it."

Jax stood up and came over to me. He then took his arms and wrapped them around me.

"What are you doing?" I asked.

He took his hands off of me and looked at me with a confused look. "You told me to grab you and jump into the creek. You said to trust you. Did I misunderstand you?"

"No," I told him with a smile on my face.

"I'm confused then. Is there something else?"

I looked at him and told him, "Give me a kiss first."

Chapter 16 Putting It All Together

Jax blushed as everyone was staring at him. "Nia, is that necessary? Right here in front of everyone?"

"You heard me...give me a kiss."

I really had put Jax on the spot and he wasn't sure what I was up to. I could see that he was pretty apprehensive about giving me a kiss in front of everyone, but I knew what would happen once he did.

Jax cleared his throat and leaned in to kiss me. Once our lips touched Jax immediately transformed into Krakalope. "Now you can jump into the creek and..." Before I was able to finish Krakalope had already jumped into the creek and we were well on our way to the lake.

Chapter 17 The Second To Last Scroll

When we arrived to the lake I pointed towards the shore. Krakalope shredded on top of the lake towards the shore. When we arrived he let go of me and then transformed back into Jax.

"How did you know that by us kissing that I would be able to transform?" he asked.

"You told me I should be able to control your artifacts. I didn't really control it...just gave it a nudge."

He looked at me finally realizing that I was somewhat fibbing to him. "I think the others can transform right now on their own, can't they? I

Chapter 17 The Second To Last Scroll

think you just wanted me to give you a kiss in front of everyone just to see if I would do it."

"Maybe!" I answered, and then started to walk away.

"Wait...maybe to which part?" he asked running to catch up with me.

I didn't answer but continued to walk a little further. I looked across the lake to see if the waterfall and platform were there, but didn't see them.

"What are you looking at?" he asked.

"I'm trying to figure out if the platform and waterfall are really over there. I'm thinking they are."

"Is that where the next scroll is?"

"No, but we have to get up there."

"Why? If it is not over there why can't we just go to where the scroll is?"

"Your father will be up there. We will need to speak to him and then I will need you to take me to the bottom of the lake to obtain the scroll."

"My dad? Will he give us a hard time like the others?"

"No, but I believe that he needs to tell us something regarding the last scroll. I'm just not sure what it is."

Jax looked across the lake, and then back at me, and then again back across the lake. "So, if I understand you correctly, you want me to whisk us across the lake and up to a platform that may or may not exist to where my father may or may not be. And then we are going to jump off of there and go to the bottom of the lake to retrieve the scroll. The last time we jumped off of there we never touched the water. What makes you think that we will this time?"

Chapter 17 The Second To Last Scroll

"Because this is your tree and that is where the scroll is."

"Oh!" Jax then thought for a second and asked, "Do you know where the last scroll will be?"

"I believe it will be inside the falls."

"The falls that don't exist right now?"

"Yes, Jax. The falls that don't exist. I believe that is where he obtained the piece of the SWOOZL because that is where I showed him how to use it. I believe the scroll is hidden somewhere in there. I just need to remember where. That was the original hiding place for all the artifacts – the six pieces of the SWOOZL, the Golden Scroll, and the onyx diamond. Back then they were all safe in there. It's also where we conducted our Council meetings."

Jax was quiet and I could tell he had something on his mind.

"What is it, Jax? What are you thinking about?"

Jax put his head down and then mumbled, "It's none of my business."

"What's none of your business?"

Jax hesitated, but eventually asked me, "Did you love him? The morpion. Did you love him?"

I wasn't sure how to answer him so I gave him the only response I could, "I don't know."

"You said you could remember everything, but you don't remember if you loved him or not?"

"Jax, the person that loved him was not me. I know that doesn't make any sense, but it's true. Even though I am remembering him, it's not me that had the feelings for him. Back in my tree, I had a choice of whom I wanted to be going

Chapter 17 The Second To Last Scroll

forward. After weighing everything in my mind, there was only one deciding factor."

"What was that?"

"You, Jax. It was you. Now, give me a kiss and get us over to the platform."

Jax leaned in and kissed me and again quickly changed into Krakalope. I'm not sure how fast he was scooting across the lake but he decided to leap for the platform way before getting close enough to it. And since he couldn't see it either, I knew we were taking a chance if we would even get to the platform or not. I think he was trying to show off a little.

I didn't want to see where we were going to land or what we were about to hit so I turned my head back into Krakalope, closed my eyes, and held on as tight as I could. It probably didn't help that I let out a little screech either.

I could feel the air blowing all around us while Krakalope whisked us high into the air. I held on tighter waiting for him to hit something and both of us go flying.

"You can open your eyes. You were right. The platform is here," Jax said. "I can see it now that we are on it."

"Whew...I mean, I knew that. I was just...well, I thought. Oh, never mind. I knew that you would get us safely here."

"Whatever," he told me and then nudged me.

A few seconds later we heard the sound of someone clearing their throat. We turned and saw that it was Jax's father, Orion.

"Dad!" Jax yelled out to him. "Nia said you would be up here...not sure how she knew that, but I've learned to just take her for her word."

Chapter 17 The Second To Last Scroll

"Good advice, son. Always remember that," he said smiling at us.

"I will," he said looking at me. He then looked back at his father, "Why are you here?"

Orion changed his facial expression to a more serious one. "What is it, pops?" Jax asked.

"Pops? Is that what you call him? What happened to dad?" I asked Jax.

Before Jax could answer me, Orion spoke up, "Pops? You haven't called me that since we were last up here."

"Yeah! I'm not sure where that came from," Jax said.

"Hopefully one day you'll be lucky enough to have a son or daughter call you that, but I digress. The real reason I am here."

"It sounds serious, Orion. What is it?" I asked.

"It's about Triddy," he began.

"Triddy? She's here with us...back at T-19. Should we go get her?" I was curious what Orion had to tell us about her.

"You don't have to go get her, but tell me why she's here," he inquired.

"I believe that the morpion may have Allie under some sort of control. I'm hoping that Triddy can help to bring her out of it...and then her father."

"You need to be careful, Nia. Remember, the morpion had control of Triddy for quite some time. We're not sure what he may have done to her while he had her," he explained.

"We will be. I have an idea to combat that just in case," I told him.

"Just be careful – and be smart. Now, I do need to ask a not so serious question...have you

Chapter 17 The Second To Last Scroll

decided whom you want to be going forward?" Orion asked me, putting his hand on my shoulder.

I looked at him and smiled and then turned to Jax and did the same. "I have. I am and will be Nia from this point forward."

"I am thrilled to hear that. We all are. Not that we didn't like you when you were Shiloh, but we can see positive changes in you. I know that you will make a great leader and do wonderful things for this land. Plus, I'm sure my son is extremely happy. He couldn't stop talking about you ever since he saw you during one of our camping trips...could you son!" he said, giving Jax a wink. He then took his hand off of my shoulder.

"Come on, dad. You really had to go there?" Jax remarked.

"What, no pops?" I asked playfully.

"I'm proud of you, son. I've seen you mature and grow in the last year. You are becoming the man I always knew you would be."

Jax went up to Orion and gave him a hug. "Thanks, pops. I learned from the best."

Jax then turned to me. "Should we go get the second to last scroll?"

"I'm ready and I know the others are waiting for us to return." I then turned to Orion. "Thank you!"

"For what, my dear?" Orion asked.

"For keeping my secret and helping to protect me – you and the other Originals. None of this, any of this, would remotely be possible without all of your help. I am truly appreciative and honored to call you and the Originals my friends."

Chapter 17 The Second To Last Scroll

Orion came up to me and gave me a hug. "It was our privilege to call you our leader. I know that you and the others will do great things with this land. We can't wait to see what happens."

"We still have a lot of work to do," I told him.

Orion took a few steps back and then looked at the two of us. "Remember, together you are the strongest." He then disappeared right in front of us.

"Wonder what he meant by that?" Jax asked.

"I'm sure we'll find out. Right now, let's go get that scroll."

Jax wrapped his arms around me while turning into Krakalope. He then jumped high into the air and straight down seamlessly getting us to the bottom of the lake. Once there, he released his grasp on me and I swam towards the scroll. I reached out my hand grabbing the scroll tightly and then swam back into the tentacles of Krakalope. He covered me up again and then immediately went to the surface where he glided back to where the lake met the stream and then all the way to T-19. The others saw us coming and made room as he leaped out of the stream next to the others.

Once back on land Krakalope released me. I took the scroll and handed it over to him. "Put it somewhere safe!"

Krakalope pulled a Mylo and swallowed it. He then fist bumped Mylo before transforming back into Jax.

"Can't wait to see how you get that one out of him, Nia," Margot said.

I didn't say much in that moment, but instead I looked at each of the four standing in front

Chapter 17 The Second To Last Scroll

of me and could do nothing but smile. Triddy was fluttering right behind me but then leaned in to whisper something in my ear. "That's a good group of people you have in front of you."

"They are, aren't they! But we're still missing one to make it complete," I told her.

"Can we go get her now?" Triddy asked, fluttering now in front of me to where the others could also hear.

"We may have a problem doing that, though," Mylo said.

"Why's that?" I asked.

"How are we going to get into her tree without her?" he asked.

I thought for a few moments. "We're going to knock and see if she'll let us in," I told him.

"And if she doesn't?" asked Kennz.

"Then we'll ask her to come out," I said.

"And if that doesn't work?" asked Jax.

"Then we'll force our way in!" exclaimed Margot, who already had her game face on. She then turned full on Spidox, putting one of her pedipalps out. "Who's with me?"

"I like this one. She has spunk!" Triddy exclaimed.

"Yep, she definitely does!" I told her.

We put our hands in on Spidox's and then she had to show off again by adding more of hers. I stared right into her four eyes and said, "Make it good, Spidox."

She smiled back at me and then the rest of the others. She then winked two of her eyes at Triddy. "Here come the Five and a half."

You gotta love Spidox!

Chapter 17 The Second To Last Scroll

For Further Reading

Watch for more books in the Mythical University series as Nia and her friends explore Forest Creek to find the truth. It will take all of them working together, and maybe a little bit of luck to find what they're after.

And, now, a sneak peek at the final installment of
the
Mythical University Series
The Council of Trust

Sneak Peek: The Council of Trust

We broke our huddle while Spidox changed back into Margot. "What do you honestly expect we will find once we get to the trees?"

"I'm not totally sure, Margot, but my gut tells me to be prepared for anything and everything,"

"You never did tell us what you and Jax had to go through in order to get the scroll."

"Honestly, not a whole lot. When we arrived at the lake we went up to the platform above the falls and spoke with Jax's father."

Sneak Peek The Council of Trust

"You guys just spoke with him? He didn't give you a hard time or anything like some of the others have?"

"No."

We kept walking and Margot seemed confused. "Then what did you guys talk about...the weather?"

"It was nothing...seriously, Margot."

"If it was nothing then why won't you tell her?" asked Kennz. "Remember...we're a team."

Jax looked at me while shrugging his shoulders. "It's your call," he said.

"Fine, but I'll tell you all once we get to the trees," I told them.

"Why can't we go back to the waterfall? You said that is where you believe the last scroll will be," remarked Jax.

"It is, but we have to go through Allie's tree to get there," I said.

"I have what might be a stupid question," Margot began, "but how do we get out of Jax's tree since we never actually went through it?"

"We don't. We head to the trees and somehow make our way into Allie's. My guess is that Jax's tree may not even be there."

"What makes you think that?" asked Jax.

"Because we're currently inside of yours or did you forget?" I remarked, chuckling.

"Oh, yeah!" he said.

We walked for a few more minutes until we could see the trees. "What is that glowing over by them?" Mylo asked.

I tried to get a better look but couldn't tell. "Hey, Margot, can you…" I was saying before she interrupted.

Sneak Peek The Council of Trust

"Already on it," she said, and then summoned her talismans to get a better look.

"Anything?" I asked.

"Nothing, yet," she said, before combining her talismans into one.

I gave her a few moments to gaze at the trees from where we were. "How about now?"

"I see an object and it seems to be near something glowing, but I can't make out who or what it is. It's like it is preventing me from detecting...". Spidox suddenly stopped talking and grew her talisman a little so she could see more.

"Spidox, what is it?" I asked.

"Not sure. I don't see anything now over there."

"We're not seeing the glow any longer either. Let's push on, but everyone be on guard."

We continued walking towards the trees when I saw Jax putting his hand out pointing.

"What are you doing, Jax?"

"If my counting is correct, I believe I see six trees. Hold on... one, two, three...Wait a minute...there's only five. Wait, no six. Now five, again. What's going on?"

Jax ran ahead to the trees. We caught up to him while he was standing right in front of his tree...that kept disappearing. He turned and looked at me. "Is this a sign or something?"

"What do you mean, bro?" Mylo asked him.

"Don't think that," I said to Jax. "We don't know what that means."

"What are you two talking about?" Mylo asked.

Sneak Peek The Council of Trust

"I don't know if it means I'm going to be erased from existence," Jax told Mylo, somewhat defeated.

"That's not what it means at all. It's telling you that you need to time it correctly when you enter the last tree," a voice said.

We all turned looking in every direction, but never spotted who was saying that.

"Whew!" we could hear Jax saying.

"That was strange," Triddy said, fluttering about.

"It was, but who said that?" I wondered, aloud.

Everyone gathered in the middle of the trees. We kept watching Jax's tree, timing when it was appearing and disappearing.

"I think I've got it," Jax said.

"Well, at least we know you're not going to be erased from existence or anything like that," Mylo said, laughing.

"Not funny, bro," he said back to him.

Just then a bright light started glowing. We turned and noticed it was coming from Allie's tree, the same type of glow we saw walking here. The glow was still there when a figure started to appear and said, "Time it correctly. If you don't Forest Creek will be lost forever," the voice said.

"Can anyone see who that is?" I asked.

The glow was dissipating at the same time Allie's door started to slowly open. A recognizable figure started walking out.

"No way!" I exclaimed "Is that..."

Sneak Peek The Council of Trust

To continue the story make sure to read the final installment of the

MYTHICAL UNIVERSITY SERIES
THE COUNCIL OF TRUST

THE COMPLETE LIST OF THE MYTHICAL UNIVERSITY SERIES OF BOOKS IN ORDER

Into The Forest
The Six
Seasons
Mystic Peaks
Rise Of The Falls
The Golden Scrolls
The Council Of Trust

SHOP THE MYTHICAL UNIVERSITY STORE
https://Shop.MythicalUniversity.com

Made in the USA
Middletown, DE
24 September 2023